Girls got Game

SPORTS STORIES & POEMS

Edited by SUE MACY

HENRY HOLT AND COMPANY . NEW YORK

For Sheila,

for lessons in literature and life

Henry Holt and Company, LLC
Publishers since 1866
115 West 18th Street
New York, New York 10011

Henry Holt is a registered trademark of Henry Holt and Company, LLC

Published in Canada by Fitzhenry & Whiteside Ltd.,
195 Allstate Parkway, Markham, Ontario L3R 4T8.

Library of Congress Cataloging-in-Publication Data
Girls got game: sports stories and poems / edited by Sue Macy.
        p.   cm.
    Summary: A collection of short stories and poems written by and about
young women in sports.
    1. Sports—Literary collections. 2. Women athletes—Literary collections.
    [1. Sports—Literary collections. 2. Women athletes—Literary collections.]
    I. Macy, Sue.
    PZ5.G445 2001   810.8'0355—dc21   00-47297

ISBN 0-8050-6568-7
First Edition—2001 / Design by Debbie Glasserman
Printed in the United States of America on acid-free paper. ∞

10 9 8 7 6 5 4 3 2 1

ACKNOWLEDGMENTS

This book would not exist without the talent and enthusiasm of the contributors. I thank them for their creativity, their encouragement, and their dedication in providing girls with the kinds of stories and poems that were nowhere to be found during our own childhoods.

My gratitude also goes to the women's sports community, the advocates and athletes whose efforts have changed the environment in which girls grow up and ensured that every girl who wants to can take her own shot at athletic glory.

And to the members of my personal support system, who helped me keep my perspective as I worked on this book: Sheila Wolinsky; my parents and brother; Mickey and Lacey (two demanding but sympathetic cats); Jane Gottesman; Jackie Glasthal; the morning crowd at the gym; and my editor, Marc Aronson, as well as the rest of my publishing family at Holt.

Finally, thanks to R. R. Knudson, a pioneer in girls' sports fiction, for a grueling and unforgettable lesson on how to write a sports story.

v

CONTENTS

Girls got Game

INTRODUCTION

It was forbidden, but that just made me want it more. The stories about bravery and adventure. The interviews with athletes and war heroes. The ads for pocketknives, fishing rods, and all sorts of other cool stuff. The first time I got my hands on an issue, I felt bold—and ashamed. Right there on the cover it proclaimed, "For All Boys." This was not something girls were supposed to see.

This was *Boys' Life,* the magazine published by the Boy Scouts of America for Scouts and other young males. The boys at my school carried it around casually, unaware of how jealous I was, how badly I wanted to share the world that the magazine opened up for them. I had no interest in *Seventeen* or *Young Miss,* with their limp features—"Rain or Shine Fashions" and "Do-It-Yourself Christmas Decorations." I wanted to read about people who risked their lives, saw the world, got dirty!

In the 1960s, though, society conspired to steer girls in a different direction. Like our mothers before us, we were expected to grow up, get married, have children, and stay home to take care of our families. If we had to work, it was understood that our jobs would be secondary. We weren't supposed to be the presidents of companies; we were supposed to be the presidents' assistants.

Those of us who dared to compete with boys—to read their magazines or challenge them on the playground— were called *tomboys,* a term that I found alternately liberating and terrifying. Tomboys could dress as they liked, play as they liked, make their own rules. But they risked scorn and rejection, and the better they were at playing boys' games, the more ridicule they endured.

I took the easy way out. I excelled at sports at sleep-over camp, in an all-female environment where we were encouraged to play and applauded when we did well. But I stayed in the background at home, playing catch and tennis only with my younger brother. After watching him win accolades as a Little League pitcher, I once told my parents, "It's not fair; I'm better than he is at baseball," but I couldn't have proven it if I'd wanted to. Girls weren't allowed in Little League then; our school didn't even have a girls' softball team.

I was always on the lookout for role models who would help me prove that it was okay for females to claim their own sports glory, but the media hardly ever chronicled the achievements of women athletes. Books didn't offer much inspiration, either. In August 1977 *WomenSports* magazine reported that a grand total of thirty-three sports novels about girls had been published in the thirty-one years since

1946. Many of those, the magazine revealed, followed a distressing pattern. Though their heroines starred at tennis or volleyball or basketball, they eventually had to choose between continuing to play sports or hanging on to their boyfriends. Most chose the latter.

A lot has changed since I was in school. In 1971 one girl in twenty-seven took part in high-school sports; today it's one in three. In 1972 there were virtually no college sports scholarships available to young women; today colleges award close to $200 million in sports scholarships to females every year. There are also women's professional leagues in basketball, softball, and soccer, as well as college opportunities in those and dozens of other sports. And fans can follow their favorite female athletes in women's sports magazines, on the Internet, and, more and more, on TV.

Sports fiction, though, is just starting to reflect the new role of sports in girls' lives. Recent novels such as Virginia Euwer Wolff's *Bat 6* are leading the way by using sports as a natural setting in which to explore a wide array of issues and emotions. The nine original stories in this book continue to expand the genre, presenting middle-school girls and young adults who learn about themselves and their place in the world through sports. Many of the stories reflect traditional challenges of growing up: sibling rivalry, first love, overcoming loneliness, developing self-esteem, striving for independence. Some touch on more contemporary issues: violence at home, questions about sexuality, changes in gender roles. By losing themselves in soccer, horseback riding, stickball, and other sports, the girls in these stories are able to deal with these challenges and develop emotional as well as physical strength.

There are poems here, too, offering the rarely heard voices of females rejoicing as they run track, make jump shots, break records, break rules. Together the poems and stories reflect the experiences of the contributors, most of whom have played sports since childhood. These women come from diverse backgrounds and represent different generations. Many came of age before 1972, when Title IX leveled the playing field in funding for males and females in school sports. Because their own athletic histories helped to feed their imaginations and inspire their writing, we have followed each woman's work with a brief biographical note.

Thirty-five years after I coveted my classmates' issues of *Boys' Life*, I'm thrilled to have a hand in bringing out a book filled with tales of bravery and adventure, heroism and athleticism—and all of them starring girls. Let's hope that this is just the beginning.

Batting After Sophie

Smack! I hit the pitch hard and watched it sail two hundred twenty-five feet. Good, but not good enough.

This time I pictured Coach Janssen's face on the ball. *Slam!* Past the three-hundred-foot mark. That's more like it.

I'll quit the team, I thought as I brought the bat back up to my shoulder. Tomorrow I'll go to her office and quit. Another pitch. *Crash!* Put my whole body into that one. It went so far, I couldn't even see where it landed.

Fastballs, change-ups, curves. The mechanical arm kept pitching, and I kept swinging, stuffing my allowance into the machine until I had nothing left. By then, Sherwin's Batting Center was deserted. I took my bat and started the long walk home.

I was tired, but it felt good, especially now that I'd decided to quit. Why should I play for a coach who disrespected me? Today was just the latest example. Coach

Janssen called me over after she watched me take my practice swings. "When Sophie gets on, I depend on you to move her into scoring position," Coach said. "That means bunting if I ask you to, or even swinging at bad pitches to keep the catcher from throwing her out when she tries to steal. Why don't you get back in the batter's box, Becky, and show me some bunts."

Sophie. My best friend—and the best player in softball history, as far as Coach is concerned. I could go four for four and turn an unassisted triple play, and the only thing Janssen would talk about was Sophie's incredible single. It's true that she's the fastest runner on the team and our best base stealer, but she's only one player. Last time I looked, softball was a team sport.

All of this is Linda's fault. Linda Allen was our school's softball coach when I got here three years ago, but she moved to California last fall. Coach Janssen replaced her, and I don't think she even glanced at the detailed player notebooks that Linda left. No, with Janssen, it was like starting from scratch. Each of us had to prove herself all over again.

I argued with her—told her that Ashley should bat second. Coach shook her head and pointed to the batter's box. "You're the one I need up there after Sophie," she said with a smile. "You're our most versatile hitter. Now, practice your bunts."

I've spent my whole life learning to smash home runs over the fence, but all my coach wants me to do is dribble the ball a few feet in front of me. This isn't soccer; it's softball. The game is all about power. I picked up a stone from a flower bed, tossed it in the air, and hit it as far as I could.

Let somebody else bunt, I thought as I heard the stone bounce off a car down the block. Darn. I followed the sound and was relieved to find a battered old Buick with so many dents, it was impossible to find the one I'd just added. I shouldered the bat and hurried home.

When I woke up the next morning, I knew I couldn't quit. We were playing the Brookfield Stars that afternoon in a game that would decide who went to the state championships. We'd already gone up against Brookfield twice this season, winning the first game in a 12–2 blowout but losing the second 4–3. I took that loss personally because the Stars scored the winning run when I bobbled a ball at second and made the throw home too late.

Sophie was waiting for me outside my homeroom. "Hey, Becky, where'd you go after practice? I looked everywhere for you."

"I walked over to Sherwin's to hit a few," I mumbled, not sure if I was angry at her as well as Coach.

"Uh-oh, what did Coach do now?"

Smart aleck. She thinks she knows me so well. "I tried to get her to change the batting order," I said. "Of course, she wouldn't."

Sophie shrugged. "Maybe she doesn't want to jinx us. After all, we've won four games in a row. Why mess with a good thing?"

She would say that. Sophie was the hero in three of those games, stealing bases after I kept swinging at bad pitches to cover her. No wonder my batting average is in the toilet.

My best friend hurried down the hall to her homeroom as the final bell rang. "Remember, team lunch today," she called over her shoulder. "See you there."

I really didn't want to spend lunch talking game strategy with the team, but I had to go. So after a morning of past participles, ratios and proportions, and the New Deal, I headed to the cafeteria. At least they were serving pizza today, with salad on the side. It's the only school meal that resembles food I'd actually eat at home.

Sophie was already at our table, along with Ashley, our right fielder, and Carly, our catcher. Sophie looked concerned when I settled in next to Carly, but I didn't care. I wanted to stay as far away from the Janssen-Sophie love fest as I could.

Coach got there after the rest of the team, with no food, just a cup of coffee. She sat in her traditional spot at the head of the table. "How's everybody feeling today?" she asked, surveying our group. "Tonya, how's your ankle? Any pain?"

Tonya, our first baseman, jammed her left foot after she leaped for a line drive in our last game. The doctor said she didn't break anything, but she hadn't looked too good at practice yesterday.

"Ummm. It's . . . ummm . . . okay," she said, trying to talk and chew pizza at the same time. After she swallowed, she added, "It shouldn't give me trouble if I get it taped before the game."

"Good." Coach smiled. "How about the rest of you? Any other physical problems I should know about?"

Our third baseman, Kris, leaned toward me and whispered, "How about every bone in my body aching from that killer workout we had yesterday?"

"I heard that, Kris," said Coach. I swear, she has the hearing of a cat. "If you're in such pain after that workout, it must mean you haven't been training on a regular basis. See me before practice tomorrow, and we'll put together a routine for you."

Kris groaned, and Coach asked again, "Is everybody else okay?"

"Yes," we all said immediately.

"Excellent," said Coach. "We need to be in tip-top shape for this game. Brookfield's added a new pitcher since we played them last. Molly Molloy, one of their reserve infielders. Seems she's really fast."

"What kind of parents would name their kid Molly Molloy?" asked Carly.

Coach glared at her. "Her parents aren't your problem. The fact that she struck out fifteen batters in her last game is. I want you all to be ready for her. When you're in the dugout, watch every at bat so you learn to read her. By your second trip to the plate, there should be no surprises."

She sipped her coffee and continued. "I know some of you are unhappy about the batting order," she said, looking in my direction, "but I think we've got a lineup that works. Each of you plays a role that contributes to the success of the team. And we *are* successful. If we win today, we go to Springfield next week to compete for the Panthers' first state softball title. So here's today's lineup. Sophie plays short and bats first. Becky plays second and bats second...."

I stopped listening after that, focusing on the kid across the cafeteria who was sitting alone with six cartons of milk and four huge pieces of chocolate cake. A loser for sure, but I envied him. He had what he needed to get through the day. Something comforting and satisfying, something he wanted, whether or not other people thought it was good for him. I wished I could trade places with him.

When I tuned back in, Coach was finishing the batting order. "Ashley plays right and bats eighth, and Randi pitches and bats ninth. Any questions?"

No one said anything because there was nothing to say. Janssen had made her mind up about each of us early in the season, and there was no convincing her she was wrong. But if she thought I was going to waste my at bats this afternoon and bunt, she had another thing coming. I was better than that, and today I was going to prove it.

We had a quiz in French, my last class of the day, so I got to the gym a few minutes late. The place was buzzing. Coach was playing the Dixie Chicks over the intercom; she thinks they put us in a sassy mood. Sophie was doing five minutes on the exercise bike before her pregame stretching. Mickey, our left fielder, stood in the corner, holding her cross and mumbling a prayer. Tonya walked back and forth to test her newly taped ankle. The rest of my teammates were pulling on their Panthers uniforms: gray pants, navy socks, and navy shirts with *Troy* written across the front in silver and silver numbers on the back. I'm number 25—my lucky number, the day I was born.

I quickly changed into my uniform, unwrapped two sticks of gum, and folded them into my mouth. The flavor would be long gone by the time we took the field, but it was a habit. I put four more sticks in my pocket for later.

Just as I slammed my locker shut, Coach Janssen strode in. She came around to each of us, starting with Sophie, to see how we were doing. When she got to me, she patted my shoulder and I jerked back automatically. "Relax, Becky. It's just another game. You'll do fine. When you're up, check with me for the signs."

With that, Coach called us all to the center of the locker room for our pregame huddle. I looked at my teammates and wondered if anyone else resented her as much as I did. It sure didn't seem that way. They were all crowding in to touch the bat that Coach held, hanging on her every word. "Play safe and play fair," Coach said. "Support each other and make me proud. Now, tell me, who's going to win?"

Everybody shouted, *"Troy!"*

"I can't hear you."

Louder: *"Troy!"*

Coach smiled. "Good. Now all together. *Go, Panthers!*"

When we stormed onto the softball diamond, the fans in the jam-packed home bleachers roared. Our principal, Ms. Benedict, sat in the first row, along with several teachers. A number of parents were there, too, although mine were both at work.

There was a lot of chatter when we took the field, with all of us piping in. "No batter, no batter." "Come on, Ace.

Burn them in there." Randi rode the wave of excitement, striking out the first Stars player she faced, then getting the next girl to ground out to Sophie and the third batter to hit a line drive right to me.

We were still pumped when we came up to bat. As Sophie strode to the plate, people began to chant, "Roadrunner, Roadrunner"—her nickname because of her blazing speed. But three swings later, Sophie walked away from the batter's box with her head down. Molly Molloy was as good as Coach said, and then some. I took a deep breath and stepped up to face her.

I swung at the first pitch even though it was high, because I wanted to gauge Molloy's speed. The ball was in the catcher's mitt before my bat crossed the plate. The next pitch was definitely low, and I let it go. One ball and one strike. Now I had a feeling Molloy would throw me a sweet one, and she did. I started my swing early and met the ball as it reached the plate, but I must have swung down. The ball skidded to the shortstop, who played it perfectly. I was three strides from the bag when the first baseman tagged the base.

The next two innings continued the same way. By the bottom of the fourth, the game was still scoreless, although the Stars had managed to get three singles and a double. We had nothing—no hits, no walks, no base runners. When we came in from the field, Coach gathered us together.

"Your defense is great," she said, "and Randi, this is the best you've pitched all year. But now we need runs. Sophie, we need you on base. Bunt if you have to."

Sophie grabbed her bat and walked slowly to the plate. She stood in her most intimidating stance, with her shoulders squared and her left foot pointing at the pitcher. But as soon as Molloy let go of the pitch, Sophie dropped the bat down. Her bunt was perfect. The ball dribbled halfway toward third and stayed fair by about six inches. She was at first before the third baseman picked it up.

Our fans erupted. At this point, any hit was a major achievement.

Coach waved me over from the on-deck circle. "We need to get Sophie into scoring position," she said. "She has the green light to run on any pitch, but you need to help her out."

"But Coach, I know I can hit this pitcher. Let me swing away."

"Not until Sophie's on second," she said. "If she steals, then you can hit."

Sophie was on first base, stretching her hamstrings. The Stars first baseman was at the bag, ready for a pickoff throw. I took a practice swing and stared down Molly Molloy, daring her to throw me something good. She took the dare, but as the ball left her hand, I saw Sophie break for second. If I hit the ball solidly, there was a chance that it would be caught and Sophie would be tagged out for a double play. So I swatted at the pitch and missed it, interfering with the catcher just enough for Sophie to beat her throw to second.

"Roadrunner! Roadrunner!" The chant began again. I looked at Coach, who was on her feet, clapping. Then she waved at me, pulling her left ear and touching her right hand to her chest. The bunt sign. I shook my head no, but she did it again. NO! The word exploded in my head. There's no way I'm bunting now.

Linda would let me hit in this situation. Any good coach would.

I took a practice swing and brought the bat back. My shoulders were tense, my arms shaking. Molloy launched another perfect strike, and I swung with all my might. The ball sailed into the gap between left and center. A beautiful line drive, until their center fielder dove halfway across the outfield and snagged it. Sophie was almost at third when the ball was caught, so the center fielder fired it to the shortstop, who stepped on second. Double play.

There was a collective gasp in the home bleachers, followed by cheers and whistles from the visitors' side. As we walked to the bench, Sophie glared at me. "Coach told you to bunt," she said, disgusted.

Coach Janssen came out to meet us. She was fuming. "What was *that*?" she screamed.

"I'm sorry. I thought I could make something happen."

"It's not up to you to think. *I'm* the coach. You listen to *me*. If you're not willing to accept that, you don't belong on this team."

My mouth dropped open. "You're kicking me off the Panthers?"

"Consider yourself on probation. I'd take you out of the game right now if I had another second baseman."

I was about to yell, "Go ahead," but Sophie grabbed my arm and led me to the end of the bench. "You screwed up big time," she said. "Don't make it worse." I sat there, fuming, angry at Sophie, Coach Janssen, the whole world. I felt everybody glaring at me when our number-three batter, Tonya, ripped a single into right. If Sophie were still on base, she definitely would have made it home. Instead the inning ended with Tonya stranded at first and our score still zip.

At least we were starting to hit Molloy. But it didn't seem to matter. When we took the field, we moved like our feet were stuck in molasses. The Stars' leadoff batter lined a single to the gap in right, and then Randi walked the next girl to put runners on first and second with no outs. Carly came to the mound for a pitcher's conference, and all of the infielders gathered around.

"You okay?" she asked Randi.

"Maybe a little tired. Some mess, huh?"

"Nothing we can't handle," said Carly. "Get them to hit it on the ground, and we can turn a double play. Then we're home free."

As the conference broke up, I put my hand on Randi's shoulder. "You should have been up here with a lead, Ace. I'm sorry."

"It's not your fault. Coach is a little too bunt happy, if you ask me."

"Thanks." I smiled. "Now, remember to keep 'em low."

When I got back to my position, I felt like the fog had lifted. "No batter, no batter," I started chanting, and my teammates joined in. We were all on our toes, ready to pounce on any ball. The first batter hit a towering foul, and Kris chased it all the way to the Stars bench to catch it. The next girl hit a grounder to first, but instead of tagging the base, Tonya whipped the ball over to Kris at third for the force. Two outs, runners on first and second. All we had to do now was get past Evie Clark, the Stars' cleanup hitter.

Evie had already hit a single and a double, and Coach Janssen headed to the mound with Carly. I saw Randi look at Carly, shake her head, and give Coach the ball. Then

Coach motioned for our relief pitcher, Maya, who had been warming up.

Another brilliant move by Coach Janssen. Evie smashed Maya's first pitch into the right-field corner. Ashley had to dig the ball out from the weeds, and by the time she threw it to me, the runner on second had scored. But the girl behind her was slow. I set my feet and rocketed the ball to Carly, who blocked the plate to tag the incoming runner. Carly got bowled over in the process, but she held on to the ball. "OUT!"

We were down 1–0, but it was still only the fifth inning. We play six. Things looked promising when Mickey led off with a single, but then Kris struck out trying to bunt, and Carly flied out to left. Ashley worked the count to three and two, but the umpire called the next pitch a strike when it was clearly ball four. To her credit, Coach Janssen was in his face in about a second. Ashley had to pull her away so she wouldn't get tossed out of the game.

Maya pitched great in the top of the sixth, and we went into our final ups behind 1–0, with Maya batting first, followed by Sophie and me. This was it. Either we scored now or we said good-bye to the championships. I sat on the bench hunched over with my hands covering my face. I had to get into the zone. But I just kept seeing Brookfield's center fielder fly across the field to catch my line drive.

"How's it going, Becky?" It was Coach, standing in front of me as Maya walked to the plate.

"I've had better days."

"Actually, you're playing well—except for your last at bat."

I looked up. "You practically threw me off the team!"

Coach Janssen shook her head. "You're still on the team. You just need to learn to listen to me."

"What if I think you're wrong?"

She sat down as Maya took ball one from Molly Molloy. "Then you'll live with it. I'm the coach here. I'm responsible for the big decisions."

At the plate, Maya took ball two. Coach Janssen continued. "You know, Coach Allen said you were the most stubborn girl on this team. She sure was right."

That got my attention. "You talked to Linda?"

"No, but she left me detailed notes about each of you—your strengths, things she felt you needed to work on."

Linda's notebooks. "You read her notes?"

"Of course. They've been a big help all year."

"What else did she say about me?"

Coach was about to answer when Maya drove a ball over second base. She made it to first easily, and our bench erupted as Sophie headed to the batter's box.

"So?" I asked Coach. She walked me to the on-deck circle.

"She said it was tougher for her to win you over than anyone else, but once she had your loyalty, she could always depend on you."

"You bet she could," I said, looking Coach right in the eye. She met my gaze.

"Well, maybe if you give me a chance, you'll see that I'm not so bad, either."

Who knows? Maybe I could get to like her, or at least respect her. She was no Linda Allen, but Linda was off in California somewhere, coaching at a junior college. Coach Janssen was all we had.

"I guess I could think about that."

Suddenly the stands exploded. I had been so caught up in our conversation that I'd barely seen Sophie beat out a bunt. I'd better get my head back in the game.

"Okay, Coach, what do you want me to do?" I asked.

She thought a moment. "There are a lot of options. But you want to call the shots. You decide."

"What do you mean? Should I bunt or hit away?"

"It's up to you. Do what you think makes the most sense."

"You're not kidding?"

"I'm not kidding."

No outs; runners on first and second. Brookfield's coach went to the mound to talk to Molloy, but she left the pitcher in. I stepped up to the plate and took a deep breath. I could bunt, and maybe advance the runners so both were in scoring position. But we'd bunted enough for one day. Instead I imagined myself at Sherwin's, slamming the ball so far that I couldn't even see where it landed. When Molly Molloy delivered her pitch, that's exactly what I did.

SUE MACY

In November 1999 Sue Macy spent ten hours driving to and from a speaking engagement with Betty Trezza and Gene Visich, two women who played in the All-American Girls Professional Baseball League in the 1940s. During the drive, Betty mentioned the frustration of batting second for the Racine Belles, following the league's star base stealer, Sophie Kurys. Although "Batting After Sophie" is a work of fiction, it was inspired by Betty's memories. It should be noted that like Becky, Betty came out from under Sophie's shadow. In 1946 she drove in the only run in a fourteen-inning play-off game against the Rockford Peaches, winning what many have called the greatest game ever played in the league.

Sue's sports experiences are decidedly more modest, although she was named her camp's Best Athlete in 1970, excelling in softball and volleyball. Since then she has confined her athletic activity to workouts at the gym and occasional games of catch and softball. She is a devoted sports fan, though, and spends countless hours watching the New York Mets, the WNBA, the U.S. women's soccer team, women's tennis, and professional and University of Texas football. She named Becky in her story after New York Liberty guard Becky Hammon.

A former editor of magazines for children and young adults and the editor in chief of the Scholastic Children's Dictionary, Sue is now a full-time writer, editor, and consultant focusing on both children's publishing and women's sports. She is the author of A Whole New Ball Game: The Story of the All-American Girls Professional Baseball League (1993) and Winning Ways: A Photohistory of American Women in Sports (1996) and the editor, with Jane Gottesman, of Play Like a Girl: A Celebration of Women in Sports (1999). All have been named to Best Books lists by the American Library Association. Sue lives in Englewood, New Jersey.

LINNEA DUE

Cream Puff

Okay, I stepped aside. Wait a minute—*step* is too big a word. My big toe shifted a half inch to the left. Maybe my heel. I couldn't believe Coach Brandt could even notice, but she did, and she's been screaming at me ever since. *Wuss. Cream puff. Scared of your own shadow.* Things that make you laugh in real life or get up in someone's face just to show you can. In basketball, when the coach says those things, you're dead meat. The other kids stopped looking at me. I could smell the shame.

That huge girl was caroming down the court like a three-foot-wide brick wall on Rollerblades. Who wouldn't slide south? Only that's exactly what you can't do. You have to stand in there, take the hit. Dad's told me, over and over. "I'm small, Jen," he points out, and at six feet, he is, for basketball anyway. "These big guys'd come and bust me up. I had bruises up and down my arms, on my chest . . . even my neck! But you gotta take the hits if you're gonna play."

He was mad 'cause I'd told him I'd had it with basketball. When I used to play with the little kids, we didn't bust each other up on purpose. Then I got into the city league when I was eight and learned how real kids play. Rough. They muscle you out of the way and they stomp on your foot and they jab you with their elbows. Mom wanted me to quit the first day. I might have if I'd thought of it first. Every time I wanted to quit afterward, what came up in my head was a picture of Mom saying, "I told you so," or Dad with a really disappointed look on his face. Four years after that first day at city league, I still don't like getting hit.

When the coach ran out of stuff to call me, I slunk off the court and sat on the bench. Nobody came near me; nobody wanted to catch what I had. I could see everybody on the floor tighten up and start popping each other good—it looked like the WWF out there. Still, if you had to choose between getting smashed in the nose and having Coach Brandt call you a cream puff, what would you pick? There's no shame in a broken nose.

Keisha swung down next to me. "Whatcha scared of her for?" she asked. "She's just a big slow white girl." Then she giggled. "You're a big *fast* white girl, and that gives you the edge."

Keisha was one of my roommates back in the dorm at San Francisco State. All of us had been chosen by our schools or city leagues to come to Bay Eagles coach Katherine Brandt's weeklong basketball camp. It was a huge honor, and now I was worried that Sharon Demming should have been picked instead of me. I felt like a pretend Rising Young Star, not a real one. And I sure didn't like how that slow white girl—her name tag read JINX—kept catching my eye just so I wouldn't miss her sneering at me. She reminded me of my uncle Robert, who can always find something mean to say about anybody.

By the time we got back to the dorm, my roommates had teased me so much, I felt better. Evelyn told me that Coach Brandt had a reputation for being really hard on people. I said I figured every coach has that reputation, but Evelyn said no, that her coach in Long Beach was really sweet and gave everybody candy. Keisha said she'd never heard of coaches giving out candy and was her coach a dirty old man? Evelyn laughed for a whole minute, and then Keisha turned to me and said, "That girl was *big*! I woulda got out of her way, too."

But that night, when the others were asleep, I started worrying again. What if it turned out I was a fraidy-cat? What if being scared was something I couldn't make go away? I love basketball. I love it more than eating and TV and video games and even swimming, which is what I love second best. I'm already five-seven, and like Keisha says, I'm fast and I can jump, too. I've got a chart on my wall at home that lists the top teams—the Tennessee Lady Vols, LSU, UConn, the Georgia Bulldogs, and closer to home, Stanford and Cal. The chart measures my height, so I can look at it and see I've gained two inches this year alone. I think about how everything's coming together: my desire, my body, my ability. I can't be afraid!

To get to sleep, I pictured myself shooting baskets, keeping my wrist loose and letting the ball trail off my fingers like I'm caressing a baby. I run it through my head so often, I can make it happen for real—it's called visualizing. That doesn't mean I don't practice 24/7. I spend so much time shooting baskets that Mr. Ashton next door asked Mom to put up a sound wall. He was joking, I think.

The next day, Jinx was waiting near the basket, a slight smile on her face. Even though we're the same height, she outweighs me by twenty pounds, and it was easy for her to muscle me aside. Keisha looked worried. "Stick it to her, Suburban. Make her back off." I tried to stay in front of her when she drove for the basket, but I was concentrating so much on sticking to my spot that I forgot to defend. Coach Brandt was on me in a heartbeat. "You're not in the game, Jennifer," she warned. "If you didn't come to play, you might as well get on the bus back to Sacramento." I could feel my face turning red and my eyes going black, which they always do when I'm mad.

But a minute later I was back to chewing on my bottom lip. What *could* I do about Jinx? She was standing by the bench with a couple of other girls, and the three of them kept glancing over at me and rolling their eyes. Keisha stayed right on my shoulder, but I didn't want her fighting my fights. What would Dad do? He wouldn't let some big old player get up over his head every other minute, no matter how short he was. No answer came. Trying to figure out what my dad would do made me more nervous 'cause I didn't know, and that was even worse than not being able to handle Jinx in the first place.

All that practice, I kept trying to show her up, but instead everything I did played into her hands. If I stood still, she went up over me. When she pump-faked, I jumped, and then she shot as I was coming down. Every mistake made me more upset, and the more upset I got, the more mistakes I made.

"She's rattled you," Evelyn said. She was the pretty one in our little group—her mother was Filipino and her dad African American. "Forget Keisha and her gang banging. Just play your own game."

But that was the problem—I didn't have one. I felt blank, like a window that opened onto nothing.

As we were leaving that afternoon, Coach Brandt called me over. "There will always be bullies, Jennifer," she said quietly. "At some point you'll have to learn to deal with them."

As she walked away, my eyes went black again, and this time I couldn't stop myself. "Wait a second," I called to her, knowing I was stepping over the line and not caring. "You have to say more than that. You're the coach!"

She turned back with a laugh. "You want me to motivate you? Okay, here's the best advice I can give: Motivate yourself or get out. This game is too demanding to depend on a coach or your parents or your teammates to keep you in. You've got the ability to go all the way—and that's not something I say to many kids. But you need more than ability to make it. You even need more than wanting it so badly you can taste it." She could see the surprise cross my face, and she nodded as if it confirmed something she already knew. She took a deep breath and said, "You need *drive* to make it work. You can have the best engine on the face of this planet, and if you don't have a starter, you'll never go an inch. That's what drive is, and it's what you're missing, Jennifer. I hope you find it."

That night I called my mother. "What's wrong?" she asked. She could always tell when I had a problem. I said, "I keep thinking about Dad. He never gave up, and he was so small."

She waited for me to go on, and when I didn't, I could hear her sigh. "Jen, I know you won't believe this, but basketball isn't very important to your father. It never was."

"But that can't be true," I sputtered. "All he ever does is talk about it." I started to say more, but what was the point in arguing when I knew she was wrong? After a moment, she sighed again and asked me if I'd worn holes in any more socks and was my hair still in my eyes. Thanks, Mom.

But when I went back to the room, Evelyn started talking about how her dad always goes to the playground with her, and I suddenly felt like somebody had dumped a bucket of ice-cold water on my head. Dad was too busy to come to my games, much less play in the driveway with me. The couple of times I'd gotten him to play, I was surprised at how bad he was. He blustered about how he'd lost his edge and did a lot of shoving and jumping around, but now that I was looking close, I could see how maybe that edge had never been sharp.

I didn't want to get out of bed the next morning. Here I was, at the statewide camp, finding out I'm a cream puff and my dad all talk and no help at all, and this girl Jinx was going to make me look even worse than I did yesterday, 'cause yesterday I had Dad to help and today I didn't. When I pulled the pillow over my head, Keisha told me she was going to jump on me, so I had to get up or risk broken ribs on top of a broken heart. How could my dad have pretended like that to me?

While I warmed up, I pictured my dad scrimmaging with the starters season after season, knowing he wouldn't get into the games. I knew the other guys liked him, 'cause they'd call when they came through Sacramento, and Dad would have them over to the house. Maybe what Dad really missed was being on a team.

When Jinx came pounding down the court at me during the drills, I stood in there and took hit after hit. I felt so bad, I didn't care if I got hurt. But here's the terrible part: all my blocking didn't stop her making the shots. Oh, a couple of times I tipped away the ball, but I could tell I wasn't playing good, and I just didn't know what else to do. My Rising Young Star was blinking out like a dying comet.

By the time Coach Brandt called lunch, I was so low, I could have crawled across the floor. Why was I even here? For Mom? She'd wanted me to quit the first day. For Dad? Mom was right; he really didn't care about basketball. He talked it all the time 'cause he wanted to connect with me, and he knew there was no better way to do that than talk basketball. Besides, now that I was seeing the awful truth, I realized that Dad couldn't have helped me much anyway—we were very different players. I was tall and he was short, I was fast and cagey, and he was more like a battering ram. I didn't have anybody's footsteps to walk in, except maybe my own. And that's when it really hit me—basketball was *my* game, not Dad's, not Mom's, not even Keisha's or Evelyn's. When Evelyn told me to play my own game, she meant to burrow deep under the surface of what basketball looked like and find out where *I* lived.

After lunch, when Jinx swaggered back onto the court for scrimmages, I was ready for her. On the first possession, when she came barreling toward me, I sidestepped her easily and snagged the ball as she came past. I could see Keisha's eyes widen—would Coach Brandt yell at me 'cause I'd moved aside? But she didn't say a word—she stood near the bench, her eyes narrowed in concentration. In the next five minutes, I trailed two shots over Jinx's shoulder, and the coach made a note on her clipboard. Why challenge Jinx head-to-head? She was heavier and slower, and that made her easy to beat. She tried to run right over me a few times, and I avoided her like a matador teases a bull. I could see the worry lines start in her forehead, and I felt sorry for her. A big smile was building on Evelyn's face, and Keisha had begun to laugh.

The third time I forced a turnover, Keisha shouted, "Go-o-o, Cream Puff!" I could tell the name was going to stick, and it has, even after me and Evelyn and Keisha came back this year for our second camp. The kids that go to the camp all know each other, and word travels fast.

I still don't like getting hit. Nobody docs—it's just part of the game. But I love being called Cream Puff. It reminds me of that summer I figured out who was missing from the court: me.

LINNEA DUE

Linnea Due has been shooting baskets and playing softball since she was five or six years old. She says in softball she learned that by capitalizing on her strengths, including good balance and throwing accuracy, she could minimize for her deficiencies, such as a lack of speed and batting prowess. She adds that getting older has meant focusing more on having fun than on performance. Still, one of her biggest thrills was getting a hit off a professional softball pitcher during a benefit game.

A lifelong San Francisco Giants fan, Linnea proudly remembers seeing Willie McCovey's first major league at bat, a home run, in 1959. Growing up in Berkeley, California, she's also been a fan of the University of California's Bears football team, though she says there's been little to cheer about for several decades. She follows women's college basketball, too, and loves pro football's Oakland Raiders.

Linnea is senior editor of the East Bay Express, a weekly newspaper published in Berkeley. She is the author of several novels, has contributed short stories to a number of anthologies, and has edited a couple of anthologies herself. Her softball novel, High and Outside (1980), was an American Library Association (ALA) Best Book for Young Adults, while her nonfiction work, Joining the Tribe: Growing Up Gay and Lesbian in the '90s (1995), also won ALA honors. Linnea lives in Kensington, California.

Water

When Great-Grandma Carrie Mae sprained her ankle getting out of a swimming pool and was moved from her own house into the guest bedroom of Amanda's family home to recuperate, Amanda's life began to change. In small steps at first.

Grandma Carrie Mae's suitcases and her weight-lifting equipment were arranged in the guest room, and Amanda's father hung the exercise bar over the bed so she could keep doing her training, uninterrupted by such a small thing as a sprained ankle. The rented wheelchair stood in the corner of the room. "That thing. That awful thing. It gives me the willies," said Grandma Carrie Mae.

This was the great-grandmother who used to be in the movies.

Grandma Carrie Mae did not look like a movie star. Not even close. She had ancient lines everywhere, raggedy brown spots all up and down her skinny arms, her hands, her face. Her voice creaked, and the skin on her throat was like tissue paper.

The videos of Grandma Carrie Mae's movies had stood in the living-room bookcase for years, asleep on their feet, in with rows and rows of books, waiting until someone might be curious, reach up, look at a title, and murmur, "Hmmm."

Each family member was assigned to spend time visiting with Grandma Carrie Mae. Amanda's evenings were Monday, Friday, Tuesday, Saturday, Wednesday, on into the rainy winter, and as she initialed her days on the kitchen calendar, she breathed out, "Oh, brother."

"Listen here, Amanda," her mother whispered loudly, "that's the last time I expect to hear you say that. She isn't easy, we all agree on that, but she's our own, and when I was young she gave me more than I could ever even begin to tell you. She taught me to swim, and a whole lot else. We're simply trying to pay her back a little. And that's that."

That was that. Dinner was different: one more voice, an added set of opinions ("Did you see that awful article about the Olympics in today's paper?"), a bit more confusion in passing food platters ("My, oh my, I never heard of zucchini cooked this way"), a bit more time spent at the table. Amanda wheeled Grandma Carrie Mae to dinner, away from dinner, into the bathroom, out of the bathroom, down the hall to the guest room, she helped her into bed, and then:

"Sit down, Amanda, and tell me about your life," said Grandma Carrie Mae. "How's your swimming coming along? Talk to me."

Amanda sat on the edge of the bed. She would make chitchat.

"It's okay. I'm okay." Her voice went dry, and her mind acted up, the way it always did when she tried to avoid noticing what it wanted to tell her. She suddenly had the urge to do her math homework. History homework. Any homework. Anything.

Amanda would not tell Grandma Carrie Mae what was really on her mind. It was too personal, too embarrassing, and sure to get noisy reactions from nearly everyone she knew. Amanda was thinking of quitting synchronized swimming.

Not that it wasn't the most beautiful sport she had ever seen. Not that she didn't like her teammates. Not that she didn't dream in splashes and bubbles, and become a fluid, silvery current as she slept.

It was the constant chasing after perfection. In synchronized swimming every mistake is a big mistake. Precision. Accuracy. Excellence. And smile. And keep smiling. Hours and hours and hours every week, and repetition, repetition, repetition of every figure.

And improvement comes so very, very slowly. Amanda had stayed at 5.9 in her barracuda figure for four months, and she dreaded seeing the judges' cards once again, saying the same thing. Or worse. Her score might even go lower, with just a slight lapse in her focus. Her mind might drift to something else—there were other things in the world to think about. She might fall off her vertical, she might gobble water—only beginners gobble water.

What had begun as a small lump of discouragement in Amanda's midsection last October had grown, by these icy

January days, to a serious ache much of the time. Putting on her swimsuit, tucking her hair into her cap, talking on the way from locker room to pool with her teammates, Amanda kept hearing her insides saying, *Something's wrong, something's wrong.*

Explain it to anyone?

Who?

Amanda had heard her coach's and teammates' reactions before. "Oh, Penny's got the quits. . . . Cindy's got the quits. . . ." She didn't need to be made fun of; she needed to think it through without the noise and the opinionated glances.

"I tell you, if it hadn't been for water, I'd probably be a dead duck by now," Grandma Carrie Mae was saying. "Are you listening to me, Amanda?"

"Uh. Yeah. Yes, I'm listening, Grandma."

"Well, nod your head now and then so's I can be sure. You're a hard nut to crack, Amanda, for pity's sake."

Amanda nodded her head. "What do you mean?" she asked.

"I mean water's everything to me, has been since I was a tiny thing." And she began.

"I wasn't allowed to go near the water. 'You'll catch your death of cold, child!' 'What if you sink in the mud and nobody hears you hollering?' It was a big old swimming hole all the kids used in summer. I'd hear them splashing and having a grand time, swinging off the tree branches; I wanted in the worst way to be with them. The day I took it into my head to make the plunge, nobody at home had time to take me there, they were hoeing in the corn and what-all.

"So I went down there by myself. I was a stubborn one, in spite of being the runt of the litter. They didn't even think I'd live, to begin with. But my mom wouldn't give up. Everybody was surprised when I made it to my first birthday. And look how many birthdays I've passed now.

"I took off most of my clothes, down to my underwear, and I laid them on the grassy part, where the willow branches hung down. There was a big old log lying across the water hole, little ripples just quivering the moss on the side of it.

"'I'll just go over to there, I thought. Just over to there. I got down in the water, up to my chest. I swung my arms, I kicked my legs, and I held my head way up out of the water. Somehow I made a few strokes, and, well, I just kept paddling, such a distance over to there for such a tad of a girl.

"It wasn't long after President Wilson had brought our boys home from the Great War. The war was terrible; it made people think about death too much. That was probably why everybody came running down the bank hollering, 'Carrie Mae, you'll drown!' They were all wild with fear, Stanley and Tucker Joe and Simmy and Lulu and I don't remember who-all. Arms and legs lurching down the bank, it was a brigade. Tucker Joe swam to the log and grabbed me and towed me back to shore.

"I never got slammed so hard in my life. Up one side and down the other, they hit me with willow branches; they were so full of panic and mad, I can still feel the stings of those willow switches if I think about it.

"I never got hit again. I made sure I ran too fast.

"Well, it's a long time ago. They're all gone, every one, and I can tell you I wept at every funeral. Simmy was the last to go. It's a shame. We were family.

"But I had gotten what I wanted, I'd got myself swum over to that mossy log. Lord, how the green moss shone in the sun. Every time I see that sunshiny-green mossy color I go melty in my mind.

"I turned into a good swimmer. Simmy started teaching me, and Tucker Joe joined in, and by the end of summer I could swim the crawl and the backstroke, and I knew the position of every snag and weed jumble in the swimming hole. They were proud of me, and my mom gave me special hugs for . . . I guess it was for my stick-to-it-iveness. I just didn't quit.

"Water was my natural element. Over the next couple of summers I got my girlfriends to join in and make patterns swimming. That's how we started. Just joining hands and kicking, making patterns."

Grandma Carrie Mae stopped talking, reached up to the suspended bar above her bed, and lifted her upper body three times, then settled back against the pillow. Amanda couldn't help thinking: This woman was a child when Woodrow Wilson was president. And she has a sprained ankle and she's doing body lifts.

And her memories were just getting going. "Well, one thing led to another, and pretty soon it was a straight-leg-up-in-the-air contest. Oh, didn't we laugh. Doris could hold her leg up for the longest time, just finning her hands and holding the rest of her body real still. We figured out how to fin our hands real quiet underwater, and the four of us got our left legs to stick up together in a pyramid. Then Maizie wanted us to get our bodies together to make a pin-wheel, so we got Maizie's sister to do it, and she brought along her friend—oh, I think there were seven of us that made our first pinwheel. We all floated on our backs, touching hands, and somebody said we should put on a show.

"Well, my parents sure didn't think much of the idea of a water show. You should have heard my dad. 'You're going to lift your naked legs straight up in the air? Over my dead body.'

" 'Only one leg at a time. There's gravity, Dad.'

" 'Over my dead body. It's a disgrace.'

"We didn't know there would be real water ballets at the World's Fairs in a few years, in Chicago and even New York City. We were mere children and we were already doing it.

"Seventeen people came to our first water show, down at the swimming hole. We used the hanging branches in our flower formations, we had the best time. We called ourselves the Aqua Dames. Our audience clapped and cheered—we were the proudest twelve-year-olds you ever saw."

"Let's back up a minute, Grandma. You got whipped? They *beat* you? That's against the law."

"Well, it was love made them do it. Don't you see? They were scared they'd lose me, little runt that I was. They loved me. And it was definitely not against any law."

"They couldn't do that now," said Amanda. Discipline was an easier topic than love.

"Oh, of course they couldn't. Everything is different. Not one thing is the same. Well, except human nature. That doesn't change. You should have seen how proud my dad was when we won a trophy three years later, down at the county fair. He propped it up right in the front seat of the Model T Ford and drove around with it like a passenger.

There it stood, riding high beside him. Shining. I had to laugh.

"He paid $360 for that car, new."

"A trophy. You must have been so proud," said Amanda. She said it partly out of politeness, and partly because she was imagining those old-fashioned girls, swimming at the old-fashioned county fair in their old-fashioned bathing suits.

"Oh, of course we were. It's right over there in that blue suitcase." Grandma Carrie Mae pointed to the corner of the room.

"Can I see it?"

"Sure. Just open up the suitcase."

Amanda lifted it out. It was more than two feet tall. "'For Most Original Display of Athletic Skills, 1927.' Grandma, that's so sweet." It didn't sound like the right thing to say.

"Sweet, nothing. It was hours and hours of practice, and teamwork, and a whole lot of courage to do our routines in front of a crowd of strangers. The county fair said they'd never seen anything like the Aqua Dames. And it was true."

Grandma Carrie Mae reached up again to the bar above her bed. She lifted herself once, twice, three times, rested a minute, and lifted herself twice more.

Amanda held the trophy and watched: Grandma Carrie Mae's wrinkled arms, the flab above her elbows, the brown spots wherever flesh was visible, and the strain and effort in her face. "You carry this trophy around with you?" she asked. It was not what she meant. What she meant was: How did you get so old, and how did your flesh get so scary and strange?

"Oh, Maizie and I trade it off. It's a joke, really. Two birthdays ago she mailed it to my house. I'm just waiting for the right time to give it back. When she's completely forgotten about it. Then I'll give it to her. Maybe I'll sign it 'from Calvin Coolidge.' He was in the White House when we got that trophy. Lordy, we've had so many laughs over the years, you wouldn't believe it, Amanda."

Amanda stood the trophy on the bureau in the guest room.

By the next morning everyone in the family knew that Grandma Carrie Mae snored. Amanda's mother sent looks around the kitchen, and nobody said anything.

At dinner, after weight training and swimming practice, where Amanda had done the usual power swims and figures and routines with her team, and had pretended she wasn't having terribly mixed feelings about being there, Grandma Carrie Mae said, "I read the most fascinating article in the paper today. Did you know that in India the place where rivers come together is sacred? Did you know people are going to go to war over water in this century? Did you know the human body can go for about seventy-two hours without water before we die?"

Hardly anyone was interested. Dad was, a little.

Amanda's evening with Grandma Carrie Mae came around again. Already, Grandma said, she could feel her ankle improving.

"Well, what are we going to talk about this evening?" she asked.

The usual tightening happened inside Amanda. The plea from her stomach: *Please don't ask me about my swimming.* And she was worn out after practice, as always.

"Will you tell me about the movies? The movies you were in?"

"Oh, those. Well, I don't know if you want to hear *all* about them. But— Well, all right, here we go. Everybody knew about Esther Williams. I mean swimmers knew.

"We girls had been training ourselves for years. We were a team, we went to meets, we were ambitious. We swam right through the Depression. We weren't little gals in saggy suits splashing in a mud hole anymore. We went to high school, we practiced at a regular pool, we earned the money for pool admission by doing cleaning and lifeguarding and teaching. We had jobs, we were waitresses and store clerks and farm workers, we lifted sacks of chicken feed—"

"You lifted sacks of chicken feed?" Amanda had never seen a sack of chicken feed.

"Heavens, yes. We didn't have gyms full of weight-training equipment. In fact, girls weren't even supposed to have muscles. It wasn't ladylike. It was unfeminine. Oh, Amanda, you wouldn't recognize the world."

Grandma Carrie Mae lifted herself three times, using the bar.

"So. We heard about Esther Williams, and we got ourselves to Hollywood and we got the job. The first swimming chorus line in history. Doris and Maizie and I, we thought it would be fun. We had no idea we would have to work so hard. We got yelled at by directors and everybody else, we got herded around like sheep—sheep that could swim darned well. But, you know, the MGM studio built an amazing pool for Esther Williams on Sound Stage 30. Ninety feet by ninety feet, and twenty-five feet deep, with miles of plumbing for all the special effects. They had underwater geysers, fireworks, a hydraulic lift. We swam till we were waterlogged and exhausted. They rehearsed our swimming numbers for weeks before shooting. I have to admit, that pool was great fun.

"The first movie was *Bathing Beauty*. Lots of the swimmers were dancers, too, and Doris and Maizie and I had to learn. We were not going to let that one little obstacle keep us from being in the movies. Water ballet had never been done before on screen. We did our formations, our porpoise dives, our pinwheels. That movie was the first one to use the Tiller, where we dove into the pool one after another in a cascade, like falling dominoes. And fountains spouted water, and flames shot up in the air. . . .

"Well, I'll tell you this, Amanda. We weren't very synchronized. Not in our straight line."

Amanda knew all too well that a straight line is the hardest thing to synchronize. A few centimeters off, and it's not perfect. "Is that in the movie?"

"Of course it is. It's no secret now."

So Amanda went to the bookcase, and she found *Bathing Beauty*, and Grandma Carrie Mae hobbled to the living room on her crutches, and they sat down to watch, skipping through the story to the water ballet.

"This is fun. . . . Look at the clothes. . . . Where are you in this scene?"

"Well, right over there, second from the left on the—"

"That's you?" That lithe swimmer, with her smooth legs and bright young skin, without a trace of a wrinkle.

"Sure it is. Look at Esther Williams swim. Look at her shoulders, see how strong she is. She set swimming records in 1939. . . ."

A faint flash of recognition tingled inside Amanda's mind. Esther Williams was not a new face. It seemed that she had always known her, had swum with her. . . . Amanda had been here before. Had she swum in those scenes? She felt as if she'd actually been there. But she wasn't even alive in 1944, she'd never been in a movie—

The glimmer of memory grew brighter. Amanda saw herself, years ago, in a bathing suit, imitating a water ballet in this room. And in a swimming pool. Then she remembered a crunching thud of terrible surprise. The awful truth for a small girl: you don't suddenly turn into Esther Williams just because you want to. No amount of music and colored lights and twinkling water and pretending can give a little girl the real power and grace she's so hungry for.

What a dreadful hurt it had been. An innocent, temporary hurt, and not very important. But it was her very own hurt, and how many nights had she cried about it? Or was it just one long night?

But she'd begun to make sense of the world in little tiny particles. One day she learned that snowflakes melted on her hand, and another day she learned that the world wouldn't stop turning just because she had hurt feelings. Is it that way for everyone? Amanda had wondered. Or is it just me?

Instead of turning into a shimmering mermaid, Amanda and a dozen other children had bumped heads underwater, felt their legs disappoint them in amazing ways, swallowed gallons of water, gotten used to swimming for several hours each week, and learned that after months and months of practice they could do things they'd never have thought possible. Amanda had gone through boxes of noseplugs, found that she could hold her breath a long, long time, and unconsciously she had begun thinking of everything to a count of eight.

For years she had practiced diligently, learning not to expect instant success in the figures, which kept getting harder and harder. Some weeks she spent twenty hours in workouts, and she knew beyond a doubt that what makes synchronized swimming look so easy is what makes it so hard: the swimmers are supposed to make it look effortless. And at times Amanda felt a huge struggle inside her: a strenuous desire to do the figure flawlessly and an equally strenuous desire to give up, relax, quit. To make every move at exactly the right moment and yet never to have to do it again. Not to have to try to be perfect—it would be such a relief.

Remembering that little-girl hurt was a horrible thing. It was long ago, but she could still feel exactly the wincing pain of finding out how wrong she'd been. And she had chosen a sport with so many ways to be wrong—by centimeters and tenths of a second.

Back in the present, the geometric flower-garland scene was gorgeous. "There you are, Grandma!" Out of the silence of the bookshelf had come light and color and music and smiling, smiling athletes, waiting all these years to hit the water once more.

"They had the camera hung on a boom from the ceiling. It was great fun and hard work both. It was 'Just swim and shut up.' That's the way we lived. I'd say that probably every single day at least one of the girls would say, 'That's the last straw. I'm quitting.' But sure enough, we all showed up the next day. I guess we all just found our own reasons for not quitting. Every single one of us was needed. We were making beautiful stuff together."

Even the word "quitting" stirred jittery feelings inside Amanda. Aloud she asked why the swimmers' names weren't in the film credits.

"Oh, they didn't do things that way. We were just a mass of pretty swimmers. You know, it was the 1940s, there was another war on. We went to military hospitals to do water shows for the wounded soldiers; they were wonderful audiences. Then we'd go back to California to swim another movie."

Four nights later, the whole family gathered in the living room to watch *Neptune's Daughter*. Complete with popcorn. Grandma Carrie Mae was becoming nimbler on her crutches than anyone would have expected. "In this one you'll see the water ballet is much more complicated. And they called us the 'Neptunettes,'" she said. "Everything had to have 'ette' on the end, to make sure we remembered how dainty we were supposed to be."

The young Carrie Mae leaped off a platform with a whole fleet of other girls, springing into the air and flying out over the pool. "There's Doris, second from the right. . . ."

As they stopped and rewound the film to catch details, young Carrie Mae bounded off the platform into the water over and over again, full of energy and vigor and balance and zest.

"And there's Maizie. Oh, Lordy, we had a good time. We weren't even safe to drive home from the studio; our vision was bleary from the chlorine after being in the water all day."

Amanda sat beside Grandma, seeing out of the corner of her eye the wrinkled, sagging, attentive face in the blue light and the beautiful, smiling, young one on the screen. She couldn't help thinking: This old thing beside me and the girl with the great legs and the beautiful strokes in the water. This smile is that girl's smile. This is the same person.

"Somewhere along in there, I decided to do just the things I could get real excited about. And water sure was one of them. It got to be a way of life. You know?"

That was an obvious thought: do what you like. But there was something more in there. It seemed to be in code; at some moments Amanda felt she was on the verge of being able to figure it out, and at others it seemed not even to exist.

Everyone clapped at the end of the movie.

Although Grandma Carrie Mae insisted she didn't need help getting into bed that night, Amanda went along with her to the guest room, asked her if she wanted a glass of water, asked her if she wanted the blankets moved, asked her if she was warm enough. All the time thinking about the two Carrie Maes, the beautiful athlete on the screen and the creaky-voiced, insistent old woman who snored. And what was that code thing, that thing that wanted to be figured out?

Weeks went by. More time in the weight room, more repetitive swimming practices, more homework, more evenings with Grandma Carrie Mae. Amanda wished with all her heart she could make up her mind.

And Grandma Carrie Mae's doctor, surprised at how quickly her ankle was improving, said she could soon get back in the water.

She prepared to move back to her own home, and something was going to go away that was bigger than the old woman who had moved in, bigger than her strong opinions and her weights and her snoring. Amanda kept wondering what it was. It was right under her nose, if she could only read the signals and figure it out.

Before moving out, Grandma Carrie Mae had some conditions: "I'll watch your team practice, and you come to mine, Amanda. Enough of this sitting around at home listening to the rain come down."

The argument inside Amanda began again: Stay with the team, quit the team, keep doing the exhausting workouts, or stop doing them. "Okay," she said to Grandma Carrie Mae. "Sure, I want to watch you and your—" Your teammates? Your what?

"Me and my old gals. Good, we'll trade. A fair exchange."

For an hour and a half Amanda watched the eight women whose bodies were slowed by age but who moved in water with meticulousness, determination, and grace. Their stamina and momentum made little whisperings to her, getting down inside, where her doubts lived.

At the end, she got down on her knees at the edge. "Grandma, you're amazing, all of you. I'll never forget the sight of my very own great-grandmother suspended upside down in nine feet of water."

"Practice, that's all. This is Maizie. Maizie, my great-granddaughter, Amanda."

"I've seen you in the movies, Maizie. You were wonderful."

"Oh, thanks, Amanda. All in a day's work. Or a lifetime's." She laughed.

Of course Grandma Carrie Mae was tired after practice. She put her ankle up and settled down with a glass of orange juice.

"Grandma, where was Doris today? Why did I only meet Maizie?"

"Oh, Doris died three years ago. We've dedicated two of our routines to her. Yes, one day you're doing what you love to do, and the next day you're dead. It's a miserable truth. And a remarkable thing. How you can be so happy and then dead."

"I'm sorry, Grandma."

"Me, too. We swam through thirteen presidencies together. It's true: we all end up deader than doornails. Life is short, Amanda."

When Grandma Carrie Mae watched Amanda's team practice, Amanda forced herself to look involved, put a mute on the voice that kept coming up from inside her, and tried to feel how crucial each drill, each element, each figure was. She tried to imagine that one leg at a wrong angle was a matter of life or death.

But it was not.

Grandma Carrie Mae watched in silence, her eyes roving about the pool, and when the workout was over she said, "Amanda, I think you work as hard as any synchro swimmer I've ever seen. Your concentration is really terrific. Are you having a good time?"

Amanda couldn't get a word out.

Suddenly Amanda's coach was striding toward Grandma Carrie Mae. Amanda scooted away, went to the locker room, and got dressed.

But the coach had set things in motion, and on Grandma Carrie Mae's last Saturday night before going back home, Amanda's mother invited the entire synchro team to come and watch Carrie Mae in *Million Dollar Mermaid*. The coach volunteered to bring pizza for everyone. "Why didn't you think of that yourself, Amanda? It's a chance for all the girls to see this movie with Grandma herself, all together in our living room. It'll be fun for everybody." Her mother beamed.

Not for Amanda. Not at all. She was going to quit synchronized swimming. Wasn't she? If her barracuda score didn't go up at the next meet, or if . . . Well, if what?

And she really didn't want to share Grandma Carrie Mae with her team. Wouldn't they take one look at her up close and pull away? From her wrinkles, her brown spots everywhere, her old filmy eyes behind her glasses? From her big, determined, creaking voice? It would take them more than one evening to realize that underneath was—

Was what?

A woman who nearly held Amanda's future in her, if Amanda could figure out the exact secret. Too many people in the same room with her would complicate it, confuse it, camouflage it, make it harder for Amanda to understand.

Movie night arrived, and with it the repeated chiming of the doorbell, the jumble of wet coats and boots being shed and stowed, the happy chaos of slices of pizza being passed. And the first impact of everyone getting a good close look at Grandma Carrie Mae, everyone being ill at ease in the presence of this antique figure and trying to pretend they were enjoying themselves. Laughing too loudly, making in-jokes, having imitation arguments over who would sit where.

Million Dollar Mermaid, made in 1952, was the biggest movie of them all. The story begins at the turn of the last century, and tells about a real swimmer, the Australian Annette Kellerman, who swam in the Hippodrome in New York in 1907 and broke the bathing-suit barrier by wearing a skinny suit instead of a bulky woolen "bathing dress" and shoes. The water ballets were longer than before, higher and wider and more colorful. Busby Berkeley choreographed the water scenes, and Amanda's teammates' eyes lit up.

"There are men there! Look! Wait, pause it, let's see that again. . . . Look at them! How many of you were there? Those waterslides!"

"You jumped off those swings? I wouldn't do that!"

"I would—I'd love it! It's like racehorses coming out of the gate—"

"It's like Pegasus!"

"Look at the colored smoke. . . . Oh, look at *that*. . . . How high is that fountain? I can't even count the swimmers. . . ."

They ran the water-ballet sequences of the movie through four times that night.

And Grandma Carrie Mae was no longer Amanda's own private great-grandmother, who had swum through thirteen presidencies, who could still hold a vertical in good form, who remembered her first day in water and remembered getting whipped by people because they loved her, who dedicated routines to her dead childhood friend. Amanda's team lounged about the living room, oohing about the movie, their voices high and excited. The room was full of warm breath and big gestures, arms waving and pointing, and in the middle of it all, Great-Grandma Carrie

Mae sat on the couch, an island of assuredness, while the voices roiled around her.

And in confidential whispers they said, "Amanda, your grandmother's so cute!" "Amanda, your grandmother's adorable!" "Your grandmother's a darling!" Amanda smiled and seemed to agree.

No. Her great-grandmother Carrie Mae was not cute, not adorable, not a darling. She was feisty, insistent, strong-willed, aggressive, fascinating, brave, passionate, and endlessly interested in things.

Passionate? Uh, yes.

A sniggle of meaning worked at Amanda's spine. Carrie Mae leaping off the platform, hurling herself off the swing, over and over again. Being told, "Just shut up and swim." And going on doing it for more years than Amanda could imagine. Being called an "-ette." Keeping her body in shape, hoisting herself on a bar above her bed when she was old and injured. Because water had an allure for her that was stronger than a sprained ankle, stronger than mere old age.

Allure.

On Monday morning in school, Amanda's science class began a new unit. For the first time in her life, she got a chance to look at human cells under a microscope. She was dazzled. A cell is a fascinating thing. Zillions of them, that's what everything is made of. Everywhere. Weeds growing through cracks in the pavement as well as the human brain: they're all made of cells. Great-Grandma Carrie Mae's filmy old eyes and Amanda's young ones. The sprained ankle that had kept Grandma Carrie Mae out of the water and Amanda's strong ankles, just waiting to receive messages from her brain cells and then they would follow the instructions as flawlessly as they could.

In the hours between science in the morning and swim practice in the afternoon, a new, bigger language began to speak inside Amanda.

Do what you can get real excited about. In all the cells of you.

What is most alluring may also be partly boring and repetitive. And will offer so many ways to be wrong, by centimeters or a tenth of a second.

A cell: such a simple thing, such a complex thing. Little-girl discouragement: so easy for outsiders to laugh about, so hard to undo. And big-girl discouragement: easy to say it's just another plateau, so live with it. What is so hard is living with it.

Try looking at a plateau as a good thing: How hard you've worked to get there, how far back you can see, way back to when you began.

And Amanda remembered what she had known all along: when a problem is too big to solve, break it into its smallest components. Big frustration with synchro swimming is made up of little tiny irritants: a left leg that tilts too soon, a right shoulder that aches. Great big life is made up of the teensiest cells. A beautiful swimming performance is made up of teensy details.

One detail at a time is not impossible to solve. Concentrate on that one moment in the unrolling motion in the barracuda, going to vertical. *Build the vertical out of the most minute components, feel the water recede as my legs rise. Tight knees, tight toes—precise alignment will happen if I can love the details.*

*Don't blame myself when my muscle memory isn't perfect.
Many things in life are slow and hard. Training muscle memory is one of them.*

*Explaining it to anyone would not really help. Words
aren't enough.*

*One cell under the microscope is intriguing. I can love
that. One detail—three centimeters of thigh coming out of
the water—is not necessarily intriguing, not necessarily lov-
able. Unless I make it so.*

"I guess we all just found our own reasons for not quitting." *That* was what Grandma Carrie Mae had meant:
nobody makes your decision easy, you have to find your
own reasons to go on.

One day you're happy, and the next day you're dead.

So do what you can get real excited about.

Because, if you do, even when you're slow and wrinkly
and creaky and spotted and you snore, you can end up
being strong and brave and passionate and endlessly interested in things.

That night, after three hours of strenuous workout,
Amanda went to Grandma Carrie's room to say good night.
Her suitcases were packed, the bar was removed from over
the guest-room bed.

"Well, Amanda, I admit I have mixed feelings about
leaving."

"Oh, Grandma, I . . . You've really helped me. I didn't
know . . . I was just having . . . I kept worrying about . . . Oh,
anyway, you've helped me. Thanks."

"I know. I saw your face. I may be old, but I'm not blind.
I'll be at your meet next month."

In her sleep, Amanda dreamed of twirling underwater, around and around and around, circling and revolving and spinning in intertwining spirals of silvery light.

VIRGINIA EUWER WOLFF

Virginia Euwer Wolff learned to swim at summer camp when she was eleven, and she's still swimming today. "It's my morale lifter, my therapy, my thinking time," she says. "I love being in water." Several years ago she took her love of the water one step further when she earned novice scuba certification. "The sight of all those exquisite fish down there among the coral reefs, and swimming among them as a bubbling friendly visitor, is something I'll never forget," she says. "In a way it made me extra alive."

This fondness for swimming, plus her childhood dreams of being Esther Williams, inspired Virginia to write "Water." To convey the thoughts and feelings of Amanda and Carrie Mae, she watched and interviewed a wide range of synchronized swimmers, from teenagers to eighty-year-olds. She says she owes her gratitude to Christina Todd of Tsunami Synchro, who put in many hours as a consultant, and to swimmers Jeanne Steed, Liz Mayer, and Elizabeth Palmer.

Virginia's award-winning novels include the softball story Bat 6, *winner of the Jane Addams Book Award in 1999;* Make Lemonade, *which won the Golden Kite and the Bank Street Award and was* Booklist *magazine's Top of the List in 1993;* The Mozart Season, *winner of an award from the Anti-Defamation League in 1991; and* Probably Still Nick Swanson, *winner of the IRA Young Adult Book Award and the PEN award in 1989. Each of her books has been an American Library Association Best Book or Notable Book, sometimes both.*

After decades as a schoolteacher, Virginia began writing full-time in 1998. Her last teaching job was at Mt. Hood Academy, a high school for competitive skiers, where for twelve years she was the one-person English department. "I kept learning over and over again from the skiing kids that when we do badly we pick ourselves up and make the next run," Virginia says. "It's a lesson we can't afford to forget." She lives in Oregon City, Oregon.

CHRISTA CHAMPION

Elm Park School, 7:00 A.M.

For A. and E.

better than gym class
better than recess
better than pizza for lunch—

not even ice cream
with fudge sauce
can top it—

nothing is sweeter
and no one
can stop it—

whenever i want
i can just stop
and pop it—

it's fresh
and it's smooth
on the playground it rules—

it just doesn't get
any better
than this—

my jump shot
as it drops
through the net
with a swish.

Some people like sprinting
there's no time for thinking
all out, point to point, in a dash;

the pistol-shot start
the lurch of your heart
one burst, and you're done in a flash.

some prefer distance
the pure perseverance
when you cannot go on, but you do;

lap after lap
try to break from the pack
but in the end, it's the stopwatch and you.

what i like is jumping
the launching and leaping
the way that my whole body sails;

suspended in air
i am loosed from my cares
for a moment, gravity fails.

there are those who like throwing
the spinning and heaving
then watching the arc of the toss;

while the hurdler's decision
is to strive for precision
to clear hurdles without a step lost.

but still i like jumping
both the long and the high
the secrets of flying revealed;

"do you run track?"
i am often asked
"no," i reply, "i jump field!"

Tennis Renegade

Out here
i am a renegade
in my black high-tops
and mismatched socks,
loping crosscourt
for an awkward backhand,
unwinding my six-foot frame
for an overhead slam.

i play loud and fast
with my shirttails untucked
and ponytail falling out;
i like to go strong to the net
and my errors do not daunt me.

these whoops and hollers
are not delicate expressions

of tennis etiquette;
my voice carries in this hush
and echoes off the green mesh
walls that screen us from the world.

sometimes these courts
seem too small to hold me;
i do not play in
perfect tennis whites
and i admit
i have trouble
staying inside the lines.

CHRISTA CHAMPION

As an athlete, Christa Champion has lived up to her name. After playing "every sport possible" in her neighborhood growing up, Christa earned her first real uniform in Little League baseball. She went on to letter in four sports in high school and then played basketball and "jumped field" at Brown University, helping to lead the basketball team to two Ivy League championships. After college, she also played team handball in international competition.

Christa still plays basketball and tennis and coached both sports at the collegiate level for ten years, most recently at Worcester Polytechnic Institute in Massachusetts. Christa says the inspiration for her poems comes from the players she has coached "and from small moments of truth during practice and competition." A loyal Boston Red Sox fan, Christa recently relocated from Worcester to San Francisco, California.

FELICIA E. HALPERT

Summer Games

Abbie! The bus driver's not going to wait much longer!"

My mother's voice swept through every room in the house and pierced the bathroom door. I heard her yell over the swirl of the flushing toilet. Three times during the previous half hour I'd run into the bathroom. I had the feeling that if I didn't empty myself completely, at some point in the hour-long drive I'd have to ask the bus driver to pull off onto the shoulder of the Long Island Expressway. Then, in front of all the kids peering through the windows and a traffic helicopter hovering overhead, I'd have no choice but to squat at the side of the roadway.

"Abbie!"

I wiped my hands quickly over the soap, then swiped at the cold water. I leaned toward the mirror and grinned. To my horror I saw that there was a dark shard of rye toast stuck between my front teeth.

"That's it, Abbie! Now!" It was my father roaring from the kitchen.

Time, there was no more time. Hopefully I could scrape the crumb out with my fingernail without anyone on the bus noticing. No one looks stupider, I knew, than a new kid with food clinging to her teeth. I flung open the bathroom door, raced down the hall, and burst through the open front door.

My trumpet case pounded against my leg as I ran. The engine of the royal blue van purred. The faces of the driver and two boys stared out at me. Smithson Camp for the Arts was painted neatly onto the side of the van.

"Sorry!" I said breathlessly to the driver as I leaped on board. I kept moving until I found a seat in the very back, alone.

It was a long ride from the neat lawns of Glenwood to Smithson. All the kids we picked up seemed to know one another. I looked inside my backpack. My mother had packed flip-flops, a bathing suit, a towel, lunch, and a sweater for a day that was already hot. Everything was here; everything was familiar. And yet there was nothing in that bag to help me feel any less awkward. I was alone, and nothing inside the backpack was going to change that.

One week earlier I'd been called up to the school auditorium stage during graduation. I received a certificate for musical achievement and the award for Best Girl Athlete. Mr. Morris, the principal, shook my hand and kissed my cheek. The previous month I'd set a new girls' record in the softball throw: 158 feet. I looked out and saw a crowd of people staring back at me. They were applauding. I scanned the smiling faces, trying to find my parents.

Next, John Mathews was called on to receive a plaque for Best Athlete. We had been buddies from second grade until just before Thanksgiving. Bombardment, kickball, four squares: you name it, we played it. And we played it well. We were a good team. But then we became sixth-graders, and late in the fall we were playing football during recess. It was cold, everyone's breath was steamy, and—as was often the case in these games—I was the only girl. John and I were on opposite teams. He was the quarterback and dropped back to pass. I was playing the line. After counting five Mississippi I did the only appropriate thing: I rushed, then tackled him. We both fell to the hard ground, me on top of John. I looked down at him, grinned, and through the steam said, "Gotcha, Mathews!"

He didn't smile back. His eyes were angry and defiant. His words were like ice. "That was luck, Abbie," he said. "Girls can't play football; girls don't play football. And next year," he said, his breath billowing like smoke into my face, "they won't let you play with us anymore."

Now we were together on the same graduation stage. Soon we were joined by the whole sixth grade, which sang, "To dream the impossible dream. . . ." The crowd cheered. Moments later I was walking out the doors of my elementary school into the sunshine, arm in arm with my parents. "We're very proud of you," my mother said. "Way to go, kid," my father added. But excitement mixed with uneasiness. In a couple of months the world as I knew it, the world in which I felt so comfortable, would be shaken up and scattered. Soon I'd be attending the huge, cinder-block Beaumont Junior High.

The camp van finally stopped. We were in the woods. Scattered among the trees were Smithson's cool modernistic, large gray wooden buildings. Walking toward registration, I passed tiny kids carrying large musical instruments, fat kids carrying very thin paintbrushes, and girls who apparently chose to arrive at camp dressed in their pink tutus.

I picked up my schedule. There was lots of trumpet playing and little time to hang out—except at lunch. I looked around the recreation area. Off to one side were four widely spaced poles. A counselor stood on a chair, attaching a rope to each of these poles. At the end of the rope was a ball.

"Excuse me," I said. "What's this?"

"Tetherball," he replied, while staying focused on tying a knot. Then he looked down at me, smiled, and added, "It's a fun game. Come and try it sometime."

By the end of jazz class my mouth—my embouchure— was already really tired. I returned to the recreation area with my trumpet and sat down at a nearby picnic table to have lunch. So much had already happened. Words like *downbeat*, *syncopation*, and *diaphragm* were ringing in my ears. My upper lip felt a little numb. As I chewed my turkey sandwich I watched two boys playing a game of tetherball. One was pale and heavy and probably in eighth grade at least. The other was darker and a little shorter. He looked to be about my age.

The game was friendly at first. They slapped the plastic orange ball etched with black lines back and forth lightly while chatting. But after a while, things changed.

I could see the concentration and intensity in the dark-skinned boy's eyes. He focused on slipping the ball past the other kid once or twice and shortening the rope up little by little. The plastic orange ball drew slowly closer to the pole. And then suddenly it was all over.

The boy's face broke into a wide smile. "Yesss!" he said, giving his fist a hard shake. The paler kid's body sagged.

"Wanna play again?" the winner asked.

The other boy shook his head and walked over to his violin case. I checked my watch. Five minutes until band. I gathered up all the remnants of my lunch and, while still sitting, launched them into a nearby garbage can. "Swish," I said, and then there was a light thud. I took the trumpet off the table and got up to go. The dark-skinned boy took one last swing at the ball, then deliberately stood still while the orb flew around. Just before it crashed into him, the boy ducked underneath. Then he turned and sauntered away in the opposite direction. His hands were thrust into his pants pockets; his sneakers kicked up dirt. I noticed, as I struggled with my backpack and instrument, that he wasn't carrying anything at all.

The next day I went straight to the recreation area after jazz class. There were a few little kids on the swings, but the tether-ball courts were empty. I set my stuff down on the picnic table and decided to take a closer look. The area was all dirt.

I picked up a ball that lay against its pole. The light orange plastic was smooth, except for the indentations caused by the black lines. I tossed it easily from one hand to the other. Holding that ball felt good, comforting. I threw it with a sweeping motion and watched it circle around the pole until it came back to my arms. I threw it again, a little harder, and the ball returned to me even faster. I slapped it with my palm and felt the sting of skin against plastic. The orb picked up speed. The swing of the ball was fascinating, its rhythm mesmerizing.

"Don't take your eye off of it."

I turned, and he was standing there, looking at me. We were exactly the same height. From up close the boy's skin was the color of chocolate milk. I became very aware of the paleness of my arms and legs, and the sensation of color rising in my face. I hoped that he would think I was flushed from playing ball.

"Here, let me show you something."

I hesitated for a moment.

Then I gave him the ball. I held it with outstretched arms, and he took it in two hands that were etched with dirt. My hands were filthy, too. The palm lines stood out where the grime had mingled with sweat.

"My name's Jamie," he said.

"I'm Abbie."

And then he showed me how to hit an underhand that sailed up and over rather than up and down. He hit a one-handed line drive that whizzed just over my head and blasted a two-fisted backhand so hard that it would've landed in the theater shed if not for the rope that yanked it back toward the pole. He obviously thought he was good. The annoying thing was that he was right.

"You were here yesterday," I said, steadying my gaze on the ball as it revolved around and around the pole steadily faster.

He snatched the ball from out of the air.

"So were you," he said, looking directly into my eyes, then casually tossing me the ball. "I saw you watching from the hill."

"This your first year here?" I said quickly, wanting to change the subject. I hit the ball back lightly. It made me uncomfortable knowing that I'd been so visible.

"Second. How about you?" He bumped the ball back my way.

"Second day. Music camp is my parents' idea." I punched the ball back. It began to gain speed. "What do you play?"

"You mean besides tetherball?" he asked while hitting down hard on the ball and wrapping the rope once around the pole. "I don't play anything. I draw and paint."

There was little talking after that. I had to concentrate on not getting beaten. This boy was agile and he could jump. I did smack a couple that took him by surprise and even got two rope lengths ahead at one point. But then his casual attitude turned serious, and my gains were quickly unwound. I lost track of time, and eventually the game as well. The end result didn't make me happy, except for the fact that I was beginning to think that I might've found a friend.

I looked at my watch and realized that band had already started.

"Listen, I gotta go."

"I guess I'd better, too," he said, reluctantly.

I ran over to the picnic table, wiping my filthy hands onto my shorts.

"Thanks for the game," he said cheerfully.

"No problem," I replied with forced nonchalance. The truth was that I hated losing. I grabbed my stuff, then stopped and turned back toward him.

"What did you say your name was again?"

"Jamie," he said, walking easily over to another table and picking up a sketchbook. I hadn't noticed one the day before. "Jamie Wilkens. And you're Abbie, right? Abbie what?"

"Abbie Wallach," I said, "and I'm real late." Then I took off, scrambling up the hill toward the concert shed.

"Well, I'll see you around, Abbie Wallach," he called. "I'm always here during recreation . . . and listen!"

His shout stopped me at the top of the hill.

"For a girl, you're really good!"

He said it with a smile, and I knew he meant it as a compliment. I even gave a little wave before running off to class. But his words suggested that he'd never taken our game seriously, the way he might've if I was a boy. Without even realizing it, he'd won again.

By the end of that evening I had successfully convinced my parents to put up a tetherball set in the backyard. By the end of the week Dad and I had gone to Sears and bought one. I pestered him all weekend until finally on Sunday he dug the hole, stuck the two aluminum pieces of the pole together, tied the rope to the pole and the ball to the rope, and hammered the whole thing into the ground. He said I was skating on thin ice when I instantly challenged him to a game.

So I played by myself. I made up little games of my own that would help me to learn the bigger game. I practiced hitting the ball with only the right hand, then only the left. I practiced some of the serves that Jamie taught me. I invented a couple of my own. These are good, I thought, but they're not good enough. I was working on jumping to block a ball when Dad came out of the house. He'd been watching TV, and the baseball game was finally over.

"Wanna play?" I asked.

He insisted on reading the instructions carefully, then suggested that I serve first. I lost that game pretty fast. I lost the rematch, too, but it took a little longer.

"Come on, Abbie, use your head. Think about what you're doing."

We had another rematch, and although I lost again, finally it felt like a game. I got him to work hard and breathe hard, to take my challenge seriously. My mother's car pulled into the driveway just as I was about to challenge him again. With unusual enthusiasm Dad said that he had to help Mom with the packages. "You keep practicing," he said, then put his arm around my shoulders and gave me a hug.

"Listen, don't give up," he said. "Never give up."

I stayed out on that tetherball court until dinnertime, then continued after supper until Mom insisted that it was too dark to see the ball. "Don't you think it's time to practice your trumpet a little?" she said, annoyance in her voice.

Two weeks into camp I wrote to the International Olympic Committee suggesting that tetherball be included as a medal sport. After five weeks I could control one of the courts for much of the recreation period despite repeated challenges. Increasingly I looked on my trumpet playing as something I did to fill up the time until tetherball began.

Jamie and I became friends. He encouraged me, offered strategy advice, and defended my presence as one of the few girls in the midst of more and more boys.

"If you're so good, why don't you play her?" he'd innocently suggest to some kid who boasted that no girl could beat him. Once challenged, I tried my best to win. And as the days moved forward, increasingly I succeeded.

Jamie and I only saw each other during the single hour of recess and only talked while wolfing down lunches or standing on challenger lines. He told me that he lived with his white mother, black father, and two younger brothers in a three-family house in Long Island City. The house was down the block from the Queensborough Bridge. The constant roar of traffic and the frequent blast of car horns infiltrated the apartment, he said. He went to sleep at night hearing the rattle and screech of the R train moving along the bridge to and from Manhattan.

"I'll never get used to how quiet it is here," he said of Smithson, where the hush of the woods was laced with the sound of flute arpeggios floating through the air and the dull thud of bare feet across wooden floors.

He was on a painting scholarship to Smithson and traveled nearly four hours each day back and forth to camp. "Someday I'm going to draw cartoons for *The Daily News*," he told me.

Even though this was his second year, even though he was famous in Smithson tetherball circles, Jamie was very much an outsider. He chatted sometimes with other kids but never about anything more than sports. It was almost as if he needed to be mysterious and unknowable. Black/white, male/female: both of us were never exactly sure just who we were. We were only completely comfortable when we stopped thinking and stopped comparing, and just immersed ourselves in the beauty and art of sport.

One day we walked away from recreation, as usual in opposite directions. I turned to look at Jamie's retreating back. Instead, to my surprise, I saw his eyes. He was walking slowly away from me, but backward. Jamie grinned a little sheepishly, then turned and sauntered ultracasually off toward class.

Why had he been looking at me? . . . Did he like me? I felt thrilled and flustered all at once. I tried to imagine what it would be like to kiss him, but I couldn't do it. Instead I kept seeing my father making fun of me for having a boyfriend, my mother embarrassed about the whole thing and trying to ignore it.

Jamie and I were pals, and I didn't want to lose that. I was willing to settle for the churning feeling in my stomach.

A few days later Jamie came striding over to the picnic table. He had his sketchbook under his arm.

"Let's go for a walk," he said.

And then we walked into the woods.

Until that moment I'd never been with Jamie anywhere except on the noisy, dirty tetherball courts. We lived such very different lives at camp as well as at home. And now *this* was happening, whatever *this* was.

As the path widened we walked together and talked. I noticed how the shadows of leaves played light and dark swiftly across Jamie's body as we walked. He moved gracefully, making me more aware than ever of my own ungainliness.

Finally we reached a small stream.

"Let's sit here," Jamie said, pointing to a large boulder.

For a moment we sat side by side, palms down on the rock, our self-conscious silence undercut by the whisper of the stream. I knew that I would never tell my parents about this moment. Never.

"I want to show you something," he said.

It was an ink drawing of a very large, precisely etched heart. Underneath in the right-hand corner was written, *To Abbie. Love, Jamie.*

I was afraid to look at him. Was this really happening to me?

"It's beautiful, Jamie."

"Thanks."

He was staring hard at the leaves on the ground.

"I've never gotten anything like this, ever."

"Yeah, well, I've never done anything like this," he replied.

There was silence for a while. I raised my head and focused on a tree stump a few feet away.

"I never met any girl like you before, Abbie," he said, his eyes searching for life on the forest floor.

"I'll bet that's true," I said with a self-conscious laugh. "It's the story of my life."

There was a pause.

"I like you a lot."

I couldn't believe what I was hearing. I couldn't believe what I was about to say.

"I like you, too, Jamie. I really do."

Then we looked into each other's eyes and knew that we were supposed to kiss now. But our awkwardness was so overwhelming that neither of us was sure how to start. Finally Jamie leaned toward me and very lightly brushed his lips up against mine. I shut my eyes, using as my model every movie I'd ever seen. There was a rushing, tingling sensation. I shuddered a little. Then he leaned back, and I opened my eyes. He was smiling just a little. I did the same. Jamie moved forward, touched his lips to mine once more, and said very gently, "I think we're late for class."

Jamie and I were an item for about two weeks before the final tetherball tournament. I never told Mom and Dad, and I doubt that he mentioned anything to his parents, either. It's likely, in fact, that none of the kids at recreation had any idea. Nevertheless, in our own way we were together, we were a team. We rooted more earnestly for each other during games. Jamie took more time demonstrating certain tetherball techniques, even though I now felt confident in my own game. I listened, and wanted him to see that I was always willing to try something his way.

But there were other things. I found myself laughing more easily at dumb jokes he made. I started combing my hair before walking over the hill. I sometimes gave up my place in line on one court if Jamie asked me to come watch him play on another. I was thrilled that this boy seemed to like me for who I was, but I thought if I acted more like other girls, he would like me even more.

Only a few days of camp were left when the tournament began. I tried not to think about the end. The future, after all, held only Beaumont Junior High. Jamie and I were competing in separate brackets of the fourth-through-eighth-grade pool. Initially this was a relief. We could cheer each other on and talk about our victories. But as each opponent fell, it became clear where we were headed.

"What are we going to do, Jamie?" I asked the day we won our divisions.

"Don't worry about it, Abbie," Jamie said, a little too casually. "It's just a game, remember?"

Morning music classes were a blur on the day of the championship. The next day's campwide concert meant nothing to me compared to this match. I wanted to win; I'd worked hard all summer long. But I knew that Jamie wanted to win, too. And as much as I didn't want to lose the game, I also didn't want to lose him.

When I got down to the recreation area, a lot of kids were already gathered around the court we would be using. Jamie was standing inside the circle. The group made an opening for me, and I skittered through, a smile frozen onto my face. Nobody but Jamie said hello.

"Nervous?" he said. The playfulness in his voice was irritating.

"A little."

"Don't worry; this should be fun."

Fun? How could he think of this as simply fun? I was feeling increasingly trapped. I was beginning to dread the outcome of this game, no matter who won.

It was best two out of three, and the counselor in charge handed me the ball for first serve. The familiar feel of rounded plastic calmed me. I remembered that I loved this game, I loved playing tetherball. I looked over once more at Jamie. He winked back at me. Then I held the ball shoulder high in the palm of my left hand, took a deep breath, and slammed the ball hard with my right fist. The match had begun.

Jamie stopped smiling after about five minutes. Even now it seems hard to believe that he didn't take me seriously as a player until he fell way behind in the first game. Then he fought back with the intensity of a champion. Bit by bit he managed to unwrap the circles of rope that I'd successfully wound around the pole. We were even for a while, then slowly the game began to turn his way. The crowd was mesmerized by the swing of the ball. The rope grew shorter; I was running out of chances. With a final flourish he hit a looping shot that sealed the game. The counselor blew his whistle.

I sensed relief sweep through Jamie and the crowd. There had been a few scattered comments, but no one had openly taken sides yet. Even so, I knew who the crowd supported. Jamie might not be close to any of these guys, but an unspoken bond still existed. He was one of them. I was not.

As we switched sides for the next game Jamie touched me lightly on the shoulder and whispered, "Nice game, Ab. I think I taught you a little too well. I brought some Baby Ruth bars to celebrate with after the match."

It was his turn to serve. I was tired, mad, and determined. I got off to a quick start, then slowly, loop by loop, the rope length grew shorter. Finally I smacked one last uppercut, and the ball flew past Jamie's outstretched hands and twisted tight to the pole. The counselor's whistle blew. Suddenly we were tied, 1–1.

Shock rippled through the crowd. Jamie seemed stunned. He looked for a long moment at the tetherball pole and then at me. Part of me was thrilled, but another part saw the shock in Jamie's eyes. I felt bad for him and wanted to apologize. A third part of me was angry that I should even feel the need to apologize.

We switched sides again for the third and final game.

"Sorry, Jamie."

"Hey, what are you sorry about?" he snapped. His eyes were hostile. "Winning's what it's all about, right? Well, girl, let the better man win."

His words cut like a knife through me. I thought of John Mathews and the football game and remembered the humiliation I felt as we lay atop the cold November turf. It was happening all over again. I was a girl who had been taught to achieve like a boy, to compete like a boy, in many ways to try and be like a boy. And yet I was still very much a girl, which was all Jamie, John, and any other boy ever seemed to see. Why couldn't they, why couldn't anyone, accept me—all of me—for who I was?

Jamie might be neither all white nor all black. But he was pure boy, just like the rest of them. He won the coin toss and with an edge in his voice elected to serve. The boys encircling us offered him advice and strategy for the deciding game. I backed up in my half of the court and awaited his patented specialty: the overhand slice. Sure enough, it flew down, then veered back up over my head. The crowd cheered, and I knew I was in for a tough final game.

It lasted into the next period. Many of the spectators had to leave for class. I was sweating, filthy, and tired, and I wouldn't give in. Neither would Jamie. The lead kept changing hands, the ball flew one way, then the other. The few kids remaining were practically pleading.

"Come on, Jamie, you can't let her win."

"Don't let this girl beat you. Don't let her."

He wasn't letting me, far from it. But the fear of losing to a girl, and especially a girl that he thought was his girl, was causing him to take some uncharacteristic risks. He was using power more and strategy less. As weariness started to set in, his swings became wilder and less effective. Through my exhaustion I saw an opportunity. I chipped a few shots past him, forcing him to move up court, then lobbed a couple of balls over his head. The rope was winding tighter, the few boys still watching filled the air with their screams, and Jamie was beginning to look desperate.

With the rope just a foot or so from its end, he and I drew close together, separated only by the width of the ball. We were straining against each other, the ball above our heads keeping us apart. I looked briefly at Jamie pressing as hard as he could and knew it was all over. I eased off the ball slightly and let him push it past me once. The change surprised him, and he lost his balance. As the ball came back around I put both hands together and pummeled it with all the rage and sorrow that I felt. The ball flew around and around and around, the counselor blew his whistle, and suddenly it was all over.

It was quiet for a moment. The ball had already begun unwrapping from around the pole. Jamie's eyes were fixed on the ground, his hands on his hips, his shoulders lifting and falling to match his hard breathing. I was gasping for breath, too. The boys who had stayed began walking away. For a brief moment I thrilled at the sensation of sheer exhilaration. I had beaten the best player in camp, and as far as I was concerned, the best player in the whole world. But even as the adrenaline churned through my body, the feeling that this had all been a trap began to sink in. I understood that even though I'd won, I'd also lost big time.

I could've gloated if I'd wanted to. I could've told Jamie never to underestimate me. But I wanted to try and make things okay, to let him see that I appreciated all he'd done for me and that it wasn't a crime to lose to a girl. I wanted him to still like me.

"Jamie Wilkens," I said, walking over and putting my hands on his shoulders, "that was a great match. You're a terrific player, and the best teacher I've ever had." I wondered briefly whether he would've said something similar if he'd won and I'd lost.

"We're the best," I added.

"Yeah, the best," he said, the pain evident in his voice, his eyes staring fixed on the ground.

"How about we get those candy bars and celebrate the two best tetherball players at Smithson?" The desperation in my voice sounded apparent even to me. I was trying so hard to take care of him. But I felt worse with each passing moment.

"No thanks," he muttered, then pulled away from my hands. "I gotta get to class." He turned away and walked over to the table and grabbed his sketchbook.

"Hey, guys, wait up!" he called to the last group of boys who had cheered him on. They were just now disappearing over the edge of the hill. They stopped, and he took off after them. When he reached the top, Jamie turned around. He looked at me for a moment, then began to raise his hand in a wave. He stopped before it got to waist level, whirled back toward the boys, and ran off before I had a chance to say good-bye.

· · ·

The house was empty when I got home that afternoon. A note was taped onto the refrigerator. *Went to see Mrs. Hawkins. Be back very soon,* Mom had written. *How did the championship go?* A bag of Oreo cookies was out on the kitchen table. *No more than four! And I mean it!* she added in another note left next to the bag.

I stood in the kitchen, chewing Oreos, drinking milk, and staring at the tetherball set in the backyard. It stood silent, awaiting punishment. I wanted to hit that ball, hit it over and over until my fists were sore. I wanted the set torn down, thrown out. I wanted to scream at Jamie for cheating me out of the feeling of pure victory, for never really seeing who I was. I wanted to punish myself for being neither all girl nor all boy.

But instead I drained my glass of milk, walked into the living room, picked out a CD, and put it in the CD player. It was the Cleveland Orchestra performing Mozart's *Jupiter* Symphony. I turned on the stereo, pressed the play button, and stepped over to my music stand. Throwing aside the trumpet exercise book that I'd ignored most of the summer, I picked up the ivory conductor's baton my mother had given me for my birthday. I stood poised for the music to begin, my arms in the air awaiting the downbeat.

The symphony began, rich and full, and I started to beat time. The music was beautiful, but the orchestra wasn't loud enough. I turned up the volume and signaled the couch to crescendo. The lounge chair on my left needed to make the strings resonate more. We needed more power. My orchestra of home furnishings needed to respond. I turned the volume knob a little higher and thrust the baton passionately. I fisted my left hand and urged the cellos near the coffee table to deepen the lushness of the harmony. I demanded, I pleaded with my arms. Still we needed more sound. I brought the volume up past where my parents had said it was safe to play. And then I turned the knob two notches more. The living room vibrated; the music filled up my head and heart. Mozart swirled through the house, enveloped me, allowed me to fly. The *Jupiter* Symphony shook the furniture, sailed out the kitchen door that my mother was just opening, tore past the tetherball set, and roared all the way to the Queensborough Bridge.

FELICIA E. HALPERT

Felicia E. Halpert can't remember a time when she didn't play sports. As a kid, she swam a lot and loved kickball and football—as well as tetherball. By the time she was a senior in high school, she was playing on her school's tennis, basketball, softball, volleyball, and field hockey teams. And although she now has three children and a full-time job, she still plays softball and is learning to play golf. Her eleven-year-old daughter continues the tradition by playing on a local softball team.

Felicia's own memorable sports moments include setting a school record by throwing a softball 158 feet in sixth grade (like Abbie in "Summer Games"), serving thirteen consecutive points in a high-school volleyball game, and coaching the St. Ann's High School girls' volleyball team (in Brooklyn, New York) to the first girls' sports championship in the school's history. Felicia says "Summer Games" was inspired by a less stellar moment, when a high school classmate shouted, "Gorilla!" at her after she blocked a volleyball that he tried to spike over the net. "I think the accepted roles for girls and boys and women and men have expanded and changed tremendously since I was a kid," she says.

"Even so, significant numbers of boys are still tortured by the thought of losing to a girl."

As a pioneering sports journalist in the 1980s, Felicia had her work published in Ms., Essence, Women's Sports and Fitness, and The New York Times, among other magazines and newspapers. She has won the Women's Sports Journalism Award (from the Women's Sports Foundation) and the Community Action Network Award. Felicia is now the New Media director for the higher-education publisher Longman, an imprint of Pearson Education. She lives with her husband and children in Glen Rock, New Jersey.

JACQUELINE WOODSON

Beanie

Now, there is a baseball field where me and Markie B. used to round up our team for stickball. Lil' Boo, who's all grown up now and won't let anybody call him anything other than Randall, would find old plastic bags and fill them with dirt for the bases. We'd get our hands filthy piling a small mound of grass and city dirt, bottle caps and stones in the middle for a pitcher's mound. I was thirteen the year I pitched my first overhand no-hitter, tall as a broomstick with a chest just starting to grow out of nowhere. The guys started calling me Jelly Bean, which got shortened to just Bean because they said that was about all I had for breasts—two jelly beans masquerading. Of course Bean stuck and later on, after I'd had my share of getting and giving bloody noses for that name, it settled over me in a way I kind of liked, especially when I heard people saying, *Here comes Bean. Somebody better be getting ready to strike out.*

Carmichael, who we said was a black boy with a white boy's name, had the nerve to tell me I was halfway pretty save for the chipped tooth I'd gotten beating the mess out of DJ, whose real name was Daniel. Daniel went off to the marines at eighteen, got killed in the war less than a year later, and nobody talks about that stupid war or DJ anymore, although sometimes I see a star hanging just so in the sky and it gives me a hollow feeling all over. Carmichael joined up with the Nation of Islam and changed his name to Mecca. You can buy a bean pie from him on Saturday mornings over by the Brooklyn Bridge. The chipped tooth is capped over now, and if no one brings out the pictures of me from back then, you'd never know it had once been there. Almost seventeen and you'd think that summer would be far behind me now but the thing about memory is, it grows. You cover it over with other thoughts and doings and even more memories. Still, it's there, heavy and hard inside of you.

Always.

Every boy on that team was a good three, four years older than me, but when we weren't teasing or tussling, we got on fine. Called ourselves the Brooklyn Braves. In the team pictures, if you don't look hard enough, you might mistake me for a boy. One hundred percent girl underneath those cutoffs and that T-shirt. My cheekbones jutting out of my face like they wanted to hurt somebody and me never smiling but still, it doesn't take much to see the way my eyebrows meet in the center of my forehead like my mama's and her mama's and the tiny dots of gold in my ears.

I had a pink Spalding Hi-Bounce with a black circle drawn on it in Magic Marker. I'd buy the ball for seventy-nine cents, then whip that marker out of my back pocket and make it mine—halfway around from the g and a little bit up from there, that's where the black mark went and that's where I'd place my thumb right before a pitch left my hand. I loved being out on that sunny patch of park with about a dozen or so people gathered to watch us. And I loved the way the ball gave a little good-bye whistle when it left my hand. But more than anything, I loved the sound of that broomstick whipping through the air and hissing a strike while people looked on, surprised as all daylight, or cursed under their breath.

We used to play it in the street, some old-timer would always say. *Be dodging cars and tryna catch that ball at the same time.*

Then somebody's mother always added, *And I seen too many of y'all crazies miss the ball but not the car!*

It went on like that, through those hot Brooklyn summer days when the brownstones swayed in the haze and ice-cream trucks left the echoes of their incessant songs through the streets. Before I learned that it wasn't really ice cream they were selling but soft serve made from I don't know what. Before the German-owned shoe shop on Gates Avenue closed, taking with it the last white person left in our neighborhood. Before Dee's aunt, Alma, showed us what a butch-pride fist was, how it was the same as a Black Power one but for *patas* as we called her and the girls she loved. Before Sueño, who was our block sissy, died of a disease we didn't understand yet and then lots of people who weren't sissies like Sueño started dying, too. Long before Sueño said for the last time, *The next* maricón *to call me sissy is gonna get a size-eleven pump where it doesn't belong.*

Before our neighborhood filled up with dying and the wrong kind of love, there was stickball.

Word spread quickly that Louella and Joseph's youngest daughter, Clara, aka Bean, was looking to be one of the best stickball pitchers in Brooklyn's history and soon after, more people started coming to the games. By the last game of the season, crowds of people were pressing against the chain-link fence behind the catcher and pulling up lawn chairs along the third-base line, yelling, *Go, Bean. Make 'em cry, Bean. Send 'em on home, Bean.* True, in that crowd was a whole lot of teenagers—boys and girls making fun of the seat of my pants, which was always dirty, or the way my skinny arm flashed in a dark quarter circle before my hand let that ball go. I'd never been one for ironing or dressing pretty. I left that to the girls who could walk with a twitch in their hips or wink in a way that made boys act stupid. For my tenth birthday my mama'd made me wear a crushed velvet dress that draped itself all the way down to my ankles. I had spent the day tripping over the dress until I'd learned to pull it up above my knees with every step. Mama'd just cluck her tongue and shake her head, complaining about me being the most ungirl she'd ever rested her eyes on. Although I let my hair grow long, I kept it simple—seven good-luck cornrows braided from the front of my head to the middle of my back and connected with a red, black, and green elastic.

Alma had told us that the *pata* color was lavender. She said a lot of *patas* got killed just because of who they loved, and she wanted to always remember that messed-up things could happen to you for the stupidest reason. She wore lavender triangles on the shoulders of her khaki jackets and as patches on the knees of her jeans. Although I had kissed Dee more than once behind the handball court at night, we weren't true-blue *patas* like Alma. We had plans to marry the first men we loved and then, after they died, we'd grow old together—rocking and talking about back in the day. Still, because Alma was Dee's aunt, eighteen, and our ticket to R-rated movies, train rides to Coney Island, and teenage secrets, I put a lavender triangle on the back pocket of my shorts and touched it always before a pitch.

Mostly I wore cutoffs or gym shorts and usually the latter was my lucky pair—blue ones with a white border and a tiny lavender triangle embroidered on the back.

The last summer I pitched a no-hitter, Puma sneakers were all the rage, and I'd just abandoned a pair of sky blue Pro-Keds for a navy blue suede pair of Pumas with a white swoop. I knew I looked fine and I knew I pitched even better than I looked, so I was more than a little bit surprised when toward the end of the summer my team let me know I wouldn't be pitching another season.

It was Andre who was the one so eager to tell me the news. Once, when he was twelve and I was nine, Andre pulled me into his hallway and kissed me hard on the lips. *It means you're my girlfriend now,* he said. *Like hell it does,* I said back, pushing him away from me and stomping out of his dark and smelly hallway.

That afternoon, I struck out four out of six guys before I took the bench to give Larry—who pitched like somebody throwing underwater and just as blind—a chance. Mike, who organized us, always let Larry do some pitching if we got far enough ahead. I stuffed my Spalding in my pocket and sulked over to the bench, figuring if Larry wanted to learn to pitch, he'd better start with getting his own ball. Mike gave me a look and scored a ball from somebody watching the game.

When I looked out into the crowd, I saw that Dee was there. She waved over at me, then stuffed one of her braids in her mouth. Dee always stuffed a braid in her mouth when she was nervous, and she was always nervous around me. I waved back at her and gave her the thumbs-up when she held up her foot to show me she'd gotten the same Pumas I had. I wondered how she'd gotten her mother to say yes to buying them, being that both our mothers thought they were mannish—whatever that meant—and fussed like the devil when we asked for them. I'd finally broken down and bought mine myself, using the money I'd saved from odd jobs I'd done all spring and the tiny bit of allowance my parents gave me.

"All I know," Andre said when I took my seat beside him on the bench that afternoon, "is that Brooklyn finally got it together to have a baseball league, and ain't no girls allowed to play."

I watched Larry walk two people and catch a pop fly. He held it high above his head and turned slowly on the mound, grinning like he had really done something.

"Uniforms?"

Andre nodded.

"A league like that needs me," I said, not taking my eyes off of Larry. I had always wanted a uniform, had imagined what it would be like to be lined up with my team, all of us dressed exactly alike—me smack in the middle, holding the Spalding out toward the camera.

"No girls," Andre said. When I looked at him, he had a stupid grin on his face. All those years and he was still mad at me about that hallway thing. "This is your last season, Bean. Your last game. You can kiss stickball's butt good-bye."

I leaned forward, spread my legs, and rested my elbows on my thighs even though I could hear the spirit of my mother fussing about sitting this way. I couldn't imagine life without stickball, without my boys and me hanging and fighting and winning game after game after game.

"If I'm not playing, y'all gonna lose." I shrugged. It was that simple.

"No girls," Andre said again. "That's the rule, girlie."

I swallowed and glared at Andre. He blinked and moved a bit away from me. Taking Andre down wasn't a challenge—one blow with my pitching fist and he'd be finished. But it wasn't worth it. He was stupid and jealous and not worth bruising a hand over.

"I don't care," I said.

"You lie," Andre said back, but his voice was whispery, as unconvincing as mine.

When I looked over to where Dee was sitting, she smiled and continued sucking on her braid.

"That's crap," I said to Andre, even though I knew it was all true.

I watched Larry, in one inning, pitch the other team ahead of us so bad, there wasn't much anybody on our team could do. Although I brought two guys home with a double, we didn't add enough catch-up runs to the pot, and the other team won by four. I lined up behind the others, then walked in a line toward the winners, each team slapping the other a "good game" five. It was late afternoon, and the sun was going down, casting a strange gold over all our black and brown bodies. I could feel tears rising as I moved to slap one last opponent's hand, then turned back toward my team, each of us giving quick hugs and whispering *Good game, man. Yeah, good game.*

I think of mercury sometimes, how it's liquid and solid all at once, and I know that's what my memory is—sometimes solid and vivid as the color red, other times muted as a rainy day. Sometimes I remember Daniel's knuckle against my tooth. Other times it's his smile that's with me. And Sueño. The way we laughed when he appeared in his front gate wearing a boa. And the time he whispered, *You're just like us, Beanie. Me, you, Alma. We're family.* And me saying back, *My name's not Beanie. It's Bean. No,* Sueño said. *It's Beanie. Trust me, darling.*

But the sound of a wooden stick making contact with a small, pink rubber ball stays with me.

Always.

Dee's family moved away the following year. Back to Bayamón. Our letters, passionate and full of *I'll love you forevers* dwindled to holiday cards and birthday poems. Then not even that.

She's getting big. She has a boyfriend now, Alma said one summer when she came back from visiting her. *You guys used to be so close. Bendito, the time—it goes, huh?*

The memories of me and Dee come and go. Come and go. Liquid. Solid. Vivid. Vague.

Some evenings I take my Spalding to the handball courts and throw and throw until my arm throbs with the power of throwing. Aches with the power and promise of some other bigger thing to come. More powerful than those moments on the pitcher's mound when the ball soared from my hand and cried, *Freedom!* through the air. More perfect.

More lasting.

The handball court's a cement wall. Some evenings I believe I can send that ball screaming straight on through its stone.

And me not far behind.

JACQUELINE WOODSON

Although she played stickball, softball, basketball, and double Dutch as a kid, Jacqueline Woodson's proudest sports achievements were in track. She ran the quarter mile (four hundred meters) and says a high point was the first time she covered that distance in under a minute and finally stopped being called a "Minute Maid." Then she broke fifty-nine seconds, and then fifty-eight. "I think just running the quarter mile was a great thing for me," she says. "But winning medals was always a plus."

Jacqueline doesn't run competitively anymore, but she says she knows for a fact that she's faster than most of her friends. She does still play pickup basketball, and she watches the pro games, too, rooting for the New York Knicks, the Miami Heat, and the WNBA's New York Liberty. She also loves watching the track events at the Olympics. Jacqueline says her story was inspired by the experience of growing up in the days before Title IX, "when young girls didn't really have much choice about where we could go with our athletic talents."

Jacqueline's books include Miracle Boys *(2000),* If You Come Softly *(1998),* From the Notebooks of Melanin Sun *(1995), and* I Hadn't

Meant to Tell You This *(1994). She has won two Coretta Scott King Honors and two Jane Addams Peace Awards, and a number of her books have been listed as Best Books by the American Library Association. Although she usually writes full-time, Jacqueline has also taught writing, most recently at the City University of New York. She lives in Brooklyn, New York.*

NOLA THACKER

My Big Feet Out for a Walk

"What are you looking at?" my father demands.

"Nothing," I say.

"You should be doing your homework," he says.

I don't answer. I glance first at him, then at my mother.

My father comes toward me. He is red: his face, his neck, his ears, his scalp through the thin strand of hair he combs over the top. Purple-red.

My father's fist slams down on the counter that divides the kitchen from the rest of the room. I have been standing by the refrigerator for five minutes now, listening to them fight. My father yells, my mother reasons, my father slams his fists into things.

The cookie jar on the counter dances to the tune of my father's smooth, red-fingered, white-knuckled fist: slam, slam, slam.

I try not to flinch at each blow. My father has never hit me. He has never hit my mother. Only a coward hits the weak, he says.

But he has hit plenty of other things that can't hit back: walls, tables, chairs, once a window.

That was a bloody mess. The trip to the emergency room quieted him down for a little while. Then he went back to it. Slam, slam, slam.

He's never hit me.

"Do your homework," he says. "Then you won't end up a failure like me."

"Oh, John," says my mother.

He swings around. His fist comes down on the kitchen table. "I am a failure," he says. "Admit it. You know it. Say it."

"No," says my mother. But she doesn't make it clear whether she is disagreeing with him or just refusing to obey.

"And you're a failure, too!" His voice is rising. "You're married to me. That makes you a failure—ever thought about that? Worse, a coward too scared to leave. Too scared to walk away and be a success on your own."

"No." My mother shakes her head. She never turns red. She never cries. Only the tip of her nose gets pink and a white line appears around her mouth when she presses her lips together. Lately I've noticed little wrinkles appear along the top of her upper lip when she does that.

He turns on me. "Is that what you want to be? A failure? Grow up and have a job like mine where no one respects you, people push you around, take, take, take, never give, never once say thank you?"

He's talking about his job. He's talking about us. Among the three of us, the job, my mom, and me, we've ruined my father's life.

I've heard it before. We've moved almost every year of my life, and I've heard it all, beginning until end, when the moving van shows up again. The next job is always going to be better. The next town is always going to be the one where we "put down roots."

And for a little while, my father is happy, and we are happy. But all the time, I'm waiting for that day, that first complaint, my mother saying, "Oh, John, what's wrong, what happened?" and him shaking his head slowly, mournfully, side to side, one fist going into the palm of his hand like a pitcher slapping the ball into his glove, calculating the next pitch.

I'm not even sure what my father does at the banks where he works. He goes out in the mornings early, suit, tie, briefcase, shiny shoes, and cologne.

He's brilliant, my father. He went to an Ivy League school. He was summa cum laude.

He should have gone to law school.

"I should have gone to law school," he says for the one-hundred-millionth time now. "That was my first mistake."

My mother isn't suckered into saying he could go now. So no one says anything for a while.

Then my father sighs, deep, long-suffering. He turns to me and sees how close I am to the refrigerator. His eyes actually bulge a little. "Go do your homework!" he screams.

"I've finished," I say. It's a lie, but I can't do my homework when they are screaming. Also, I'm hungry, although it's nowhere near time for dinner. That's why I was at the refrigerator in the first place, hoping to sneak out an apple, some cheese, something.

But I can't now. My father doesn't like it when I "stand in front of the refrigerator and graze like a cow." Aren't I big enough? he says. If I'd eat right, he says, I wouldn't be so hungry all the time.

"She's a growing girl," my mother says.

Duh.

I'm taller than my mom. Almost as tall as my dad. I'm not even a little fat. But I am big. I have big hands and big ears and really big feet, so big that even as tall as I am, they look borrowed from someone even bigger.

My feet annoy my father a lot. They've grown even faster than I have. I've had to get new shoes three times this year. The ones I'm wearing now, sneakers still new enough to look new, feel tight and hot.

I have a little of my allowance left. It's the world's smallest allowance, but if I want more money I should get a job, only who would hire me, according to my father. I'm trying to save it, I don't know why, but now I think maybe I'll spend some, go get something to eat. Fries. A salad. A smoothie.

My mouth begins to water.

"I think I'll go for a walk," I say.

He spins and his fist comes down on the little bookcase next to the counter. Two cookbooks jump off onto the floor, and he glares at them. "Cheap piece of garbage," he says, and hits the bookcase again.

He's never hit me.

Not yet.

I edge out of the kitchen.

"Go ahead," he says. "Go for a walk. Get out of here. Use your big feet instead of your big mouth for a change."

"John," says my mother, tight-lipped, white-lipped.

He jerks around, and I head for the front door. As I open it, he shouts after me, "That's right. Wear out the shoe leather. Next time you buy your own shoes, Bigfoot."

I slam the door behind me, hard as a fist.

The late afternoon light of early fall spatters the sidewalk, gold poured from the paint can of the sky through the trees. The leaves are turning colors, too. They wave, preen; don't know that this is it, their last big turnout before the burnout, the falling leaf dirt dance.

I shuffle along, watching where I put my big feet. I'm clumsy. My father's right about that. Cobbled together a little wrong, so that my feet trip on things I don't see, my hands drop dishes, books, cans of soda.

I'll grow out of it, my mother says.

When? Not soon enough.

Meanwhile I'm trying to keep a low profile at this new school, in this new town; hard enough when you tower over most of your classmates, harder still when you trip over the book you just dropped on the floor, for example, while you are trying to pick it up.

Oh, well, I tell myself. We'll probably be gone by spring anyway.

And then I think, In four more springs, I can go. I'm twelve going on thirteen. I can drop out of school when I'm sixteen, leave home.

The thought scares me. I push it away and keep walking.

I'm at the park before I know it. I turn in, staying on the main paths, not looking at the stupid happy people going by, couples and parents with kids riding on their shoulders, in strollers, on training wheel bikes.

My father was pretty angry when I couldn't get the hang of bike riding right away. "Anyone can do it!" he kept shouting.

"John, she's only six," my mother kept saying.

"I was busting pavement when I was her age," he'd retort, and lift me up from the tangle of pedal and frame, crying.

I learned not to cry.

Eventually, when he wasn't around, I learned to ride the bike. I rode my bike everywhere after that, far, far away from the noise inside my house.

But lately, I'm ashamed to be seen on my bike. It's too small.

I'm too big.

The sun strikes something white and shiny in the tall grass at the edge of the field. A bird? A plastic bag left by one of the happy stupid litterbug people?

I walk over to it.

It's a soccer ball. Black and white. Scuffed. A patch missing from one of the five-sided patches out of which it is made.

I pick it up and drop it and kick it.

To my surprise, it rolls evenly.

I've played soccer at every school I've been at, of course. I've also played kickball, softball, basketball, volleyball, and a bunch of other silly games. I never stayed anywhere long enough to get good. I never stayed anywhere long enough to join a team even if I wasn't the klutz of the world.

Looking around, I wait for someone to come claim the ball. I wait for some snot-nosed kid followed by a beaming dad, a proud mom, to come zooming toward me shouting, "MINE, MINE, MINE."

No one comes.

I kick the ball again. I jog after it, like I've seen good players do. I kick it, I jog. I kick it, I jog.

It's hard work. I stumble more than once, kick the ball badly most of the time. But I don't quit. I just keep kicking that old ball, following it wherever it leads me.

Eventually we come, the ball and I, to a low stone wall. I kick the ball hard and it smashes into the wall. It rebounds straight back at me.

Almost without thinking, I step back and kick it again.

To my amazement, my foot connects and the ball goes straight and true, back to the wall and then back to me.

After that we begin to dance, the ball and I. I kick it at the wall, my stone-silent opponent, and the wall sends the ball to me, sometimes true, sometimes curving sideways or rising up or skittering. I lose it, chase it, guide it back, kick it against the wall again.

I lose all track of time, until I realize it is so dark, I can barely see the ball, that the last of the families are drifting by.

Time to go.

Time to go back.

"Come on," says the girl. I recognize her from math— Marthe, pronounced Marta, I think.

"Come on!" she shouts again, and runs past, the ball at the tips of her cleats and then sailing high in the air to another girl in the middle of the field.

I step from the sidelines into the game on the school-yard soccer field. The jocks play soccer every chance they get. Sometimes others join in, but I never have.

I run along with the rest of the swirling, jostling players, not sure what to do. I try to avoid colliding with anyone.

And then it's there. The ball. I kick it once, I kick it twice, following it, looking up.

"Over here, over here," a girl with dark hair in a swinging ponytail shouts, her hand a flag, and just like that I kick it to her.

She touches it once, passes it long, and is gone.

"Keep going," Marthe shouts, sprinting past me. "You can't just pass and stand still."

I follow her, running without thinking, without tripping. I pull alongside her.

"Go wing!" she orders, and I run away from the sweep of her arm, as if I understand what she means. We are close to the goal now. Everyone's scrambling, kicking, shouting; dust boils up around us.

The ball comes out of the slap and stomp of feet and Marthe takes it with the side of her foot, dodges left, right, left. The girl who is trying to take it away from her gets caught flat-footed, then turns and is after Marthe, bumping Marthe with her hip, her shoulder, stabbing at the ball with her toe.

Calmly Marthe looks up, sees me, still rooted where she told me to go.

She kicks it to me, a neat little pass like the ball has a magnet in it and my foot does, too.

I stop it like I've stopped it a thousand times these last few weeks on my walks out of my father's rage, my family's house.

"Put it up!" Marthe shouts.

"Take the shot!" someone screams.

"Block the shot!" someone else screams louder.

And I kick it at the goal. It goes up and toward it, and I stand in amazement as the goalie just gets it, just barely.

Marthe nods. "Not bad," she says.

I play the whole game, until it is time to go back to class.

At the end Marthe says, "You should come out and practice with the team. Maybe think about trying out, really learning the game. You might not make the team right away, probably, but you'd make the reserve team, have a chance to really get suckered into soccer insanity."

She smiles, a big smile full of pure soccer love and joy.

I shrug.

"Every afternoon, right over there," she continues, motioning not with her hand, but with her foot.

"Maybe," I say.

"Think it over," she says. "I'll be there. I'll tell the coach who you are."

I look at her in surprise. How does she know who I am? I've never spoken to her.

Her eyes light up and she smiles even more. "It's a great game," she says. "The best game in the world."

"What do I need to bring?" I ask then.

"Bring your feet," she says. "That's all."

"Where've you been?" asks my mother.

I shrug.

"You're a mess." My father emerges from his study. "What happened to you? Look at your clothes."

I've been playing soccer with the team at school in my jeans and my sneakers, which no longer look new. I'm covered in dirt and grass stains and I'm tired all over.

For a moment I think of telling him. My father was an athlete in college. Track and field, with trophies to prove it. Maybe he'd be proud of me.

But I shake off the impulse to share. Information is power, my father says, and I listen when he shouts.

"Look at her," he says to my mother, and his face starts turning crimson.

"I fell off my bike," I say.

"Are you hurt?" my mother says.

"No one hit you?" my father demands at the same moment. "I'll kill any maniac driver that hit you. We'll sue."

"No," I say. "No one hit me. I'm fine."

"Oh," my father says. "Well, you better not break that bike. We can't afford a new one."

"Fine," I say.

I go to my room and lie down on my bed and breathe.

The shouting is louder than I've ever heard it. I wake up from an unplanned nap and my stomach is rumbling and my father is shouting, "Do you? Well, do you?"

I shuffle down the hall and into the kitchen.

He turns like a prizefighter, his hand coming up.

My mother cries, "John, no!"

The hand smashes into the wall right next to my head, so close, I feel the breeze of it on my ear. I hear plaster shake loose inside the wall.

I hear something in my own brain shake loose.

"Look at you," my father says. "You're a mess."

Our eyes lock. His are bloodshot, maddened, the pupils expanding and contracting.

Our eyes are the same color: we look alike, my father and I. And I can feel the red coming up my neck, my face, filling my eyes with rage.

My mother is hovering.

I stare at my dad. I could make him hit me; I have the power right now, right at this moment. And if he hit me, he'd be sorry, and then he'd behave better.

At least for a while, the way he used to be when he hit things and broke them—until we all got used to it.

We all wait. He is breathing so hard.

I am not breathing at all. I want to hit him and make him hit me. I want to start this fight that I will, in the end, lose. I want him to throw me out of the house. I want to run away. I want him to say I'm sorry; I want to make him pay. I could do it. I could.

At last I lower my eyes. I say, "I guess I'll go for a walk," and I slide away from the fist resting in the cup it's made for itself in the wall next to my head.

"You do that," my father says, his breath coming through his clenched teeth in a whistle. "Go. Get out of here. Walk around town looking like that, and let the whole world see what a slob you are."

I pick up my pack and ease out the door. The soccer ball, dirty white and missing three patches now, is in the bottom of the pack.

When I get to the corner, I take the ball out and drop it on the ground at the edge of the sidewalk and begin to dribble toward the park, jogging slowly, concentrating on using my foot to control the ball, inside, outside, on the laces, on the toes, the way the coach showed me.

I have almost enough money saved up for a pair of cleats. A pair of cleats is essential if I want to try out for the team.

And I want that. I want to play. I can do this. I can make the team. I'm good for a beginner. I knew it even without the coach saying so. I can practice and get better and better. And if I can make the team here, I can make the team anywhere my mother and father take me.

I am not my father. I am not my mother.

I am me. And I am going to be a soccer player.

The world is at my big feet.

NOLA THACKER

Nola Thacker points to the experience of playing for her university's club soccer team as her proudest athletic achievement. Indeed, soccer has been part of her life since she first got involved in the game as a teenager in Alabama. Not only does she still play today, she also coaches a team in Brooklyn, New York, part of the New York Metropolitan Women's Soccer League. Nola says "My Big Feet Out for a Walk" was inspired by "what I learned from the people I played soccer for and with and the players on the teams I've coached."

Not surprisingly, Nola is a fan of the U.S. women's soccer team, as well as the Italian and Brazilian men's and women's soccer leagues and the WNBA's New York Liberty basketball team. When she's not involved in soccer, she's biking, hiking, cross-country skiing—and reading.

A full-time writer, Nola publishes books under her own name and a few pseudonyms. Her first middle-grade book, Summer Stories, *won the Alabama Library Association Award. She lives in Sag Harbor, New York.*

NANCY BOUTILIER

What the Cat Contemplates While Pretending to Clean Herself

o attentive
to her paws
she seems
leaning over
licking
tirelessly
but thinking
not about what dirt
has climbed under her claws.
No, the cat sees herself
sternly stepping to the plate
spitting in her paw palms
and gripping the bat just so.
With a look of feline indifference
she tends to one final itch

before staring down the pitcher
in the last instant before delivery.

When she rubs
her wet cat wrist
behind her furry ear
you'd think she had a spot
of mud there
or a flea
but really
the cat is signaling
the runner at first
to stretch that lead a little further down the baseline.

By the time
she is perched
on her hind legs
lapping at the fur
of her underside
the cat is sliding safely
into home.

The Rhythm of Strong

"Harder on port!"
"Don't shoot your slide!"
"Your stroke is too short!"
"Give it more glide!"

"A little less layback,
now raise your hands . . ."
I cannot keep track
of my coach's demands,
but I keep on rowing
though my whole body aches.
I just keep doing
whatever it takes
to remain in sync
and keep the boat aligned.

I am just one link
in this eight-woman spine.

"A cleaner catch!"
"Don't let the blade dive!"
"Not so much splash!"
"Stronger leg drive!"

We all try to hear
our coach's commands,
but a rower's ear
has other plans.
As the body resounds
with the pulse of the stroke,
the ear attunes to sounds
within the boat.
You can hear the water's chop,
a late oar drop,
a teammate regripping,
or just her sweat dripping.
The rhythm of strong
is what rowers discover,
the body's song
of pull and recover.
The first time you hear it,
it's a little bit frightening,
then you silently cheer it:
the music of muscle tightening.
An eight-oared symphony
as our strokes hit one stride—

a whole new harmony,
a whole new ride.
We become our blades.
We become their feather.
All else fades
when eight hearts pull together.

NANCY BOUTILIER

Nancy Boutilier has run—and finished—the Boston Marathon; rowed in Boston's Head of the Charles regatta; guarded Hall of Fame basketball player Ann Meyers in a pickup game; and competed in just about every sport imaginable, including volleyball, basketball, and softball in high school, and lacrosse, basketball, softball, and rowing in college. She grew up loving the Boston Celtics and Red Sox and rooting for tennis legend Billie Jean King. More recently, she was a big fan of the San Jose Lasers of the American Basketball League, the pro league that made its mark in two and a half memorable seasons from 1996 through 1998.

Nancy has published two collections of poetry, and her poems and short stories have appeared in a variety of publications and anthologies. She lives in San Francisco, California, where she is athletic director and girls' basketball coach at San Francisco University High School.

LUCY JANE BLEDSOE

Rough Touch

uthie wasn't hungry for breakfast. She dreaded her race that afternoon. She hated track and field. It was the worst sport. You're by yourself. They see you. They see all of you. They see you come in last. In a race, there was only a starting line, running bodies, and a finish line. There was no way to lose yourself.

"You have to eat," her mom said, so Ruthie poured the skim milk on her sugarless cereal and looked into the bowl.

"Which event are you doing?" her mom asked too cheerfully.

"Fifteen hundred meter." Those three words felt like icy stones in Ruthie's mouth.

"You should be running the hundred meter. You have sprinter's genes."

Ruthie's mom had been saying this every day all fall. *You have sprinter's genes.* Without even looking, Ruthie could see her mom's blue ribbons billowing, as if they were flag sized, in the glass cabinet behind the kitchen table. She could also picture perfectly the photograph next to the ribbons, her mom's arms raised over her head as her chest busted through the finish-line tape. She could see her mom's short hair, wet with sweat and victory, her long limbs, stringy with perfectly tuned muscles.

"I want to quit the track team," Ruthie said.

"Oh, honey." Her mom softened and began rebraiding Ruthie's hair. "Give it one season. By the end of the year, you'll love running. You'll feel so good about yourself once you slim down."

Her mother finally went upstairs to dress for work, and Ruthie dumped her soggy cereal down the garbage disposal. She grabbed her gym bag and left the house without saying good-bye, slamming the door. As she walked to school, she crawled deep into her body, as if it were a cave where she could hide. Inside there, she could be anyone she wanted to be. Inside there, she could wander for hours and no one would bother her. Sometimes she liked that feeling, but other times she felt too alone. She wanted out and couldn't find the passageway.

Ruthie kicked the crispy brown and yellow leaves as she walked, hoping for a miracle that would cancel the track-and-field meet. A torrential storm. A massive traffic jam that prevented the other team from getting to her school. Maybe she could sprain her ankle.

None of those things happened, though, by the time she reached the entrance to her school. As she entered the building, Ruthie pressed her books against her chest as if they were a football. She pretended the hallway was a field, a hundred yards long and fifty wide. All the kids pushing toward her, shoving past her, were her opponents. The door of her classroom was the goal line. If she could get there without encountering Joel Woodbridge, she would score a touchdown.

When her classroom was just ten yards away, she thought of raising her books over her head and prancing, her knees high, like the pros did when they crossed the goal line for a touchdown. It wouldn't matter if she did that. Everyone already thought she was weird. But she kept the books plastered to her chest. She kept moving down the hall. Five yards to go. Three yards.

Joel Woodbridge blocked her way. "Boom!" he said. "Flat on their faces. Come on, Ruthie. You'd be the best tackle in the school."

Every day a group of boys played pickup football after school. And every day Joel asked Ruthie to block for him. Of course, he was taunting her, making fun of her being fat, but he always said it as a mock compliment. "You'd be awesome. *No* one could get around *you*."

Usually when Ruthie saw Joel's white-blond head and jutting red ears coming down the hall, she tried to avoid him. No one could stand Joel. He was mean. He enjoyed annoying people. He was always smart-mouthing. Ruthie didn't want anyone to think that she was friends with him. But here was the problem: Joel shared her passion for football. Sometimes, even though she knew he was taunting her, even though she knew they probably wouldn't really let her, she considered his offer to play football with the boys. She wanted to play so badly. The mud and grass stains. The hard, cold air. The rough touch.

Today he stood in her path, his eyes all wild and flashing, and asked her, "Hey, Ruthie, did ya see that play last night?"

She couldn't help smiling. It was that perfect forty-three-yard pass that won the game for the Niners. Unfortunately, right after the quarterback hauled back his arm and let fly, her mother appeared in the doorway of the family room and began nagging her about eating Red Vines the night before a track meet. "Shhh," Ruthie had said as she watched the spiraling football reach the apex of its flight. She loved the way it looked against the cold night sky and then, as it began to descend, against the bright green Astro-Turf. She loved watching the fluid legs of the wide receiver run toward the ball's destination. The way his hands reached out, just barely catching the pass the second after he crossed the goal line. She loved the roaring fans, the team hugs, the commentators' pumped-up voices. She loved the slow-motion instant replays.

"Ruthie, I'm *talking* to you," her mother said two more times.

If only Ruthie could disappear into that perfect pass and catch. If only, for just a moment even, she could *become* that perfectly spinning football.

That was the thing about Joel Woodbridge. He was obnoxious. But he understood *that* about football. Still, she didn't want anyone seeing her talking to Joel. So she stepped around him and entered the classroom.

"Ka-*boom*," he said to her back. "You'd flatten the whole defense."

After school, Ruthie walked slowly to the track for her meet. A few minutes later, she stood on the starting line with the other girls. The sky was dark, almost purple, and an irregular wind tossed a hamburger carton across the runners' lanes. The starting gun fired. Cold air raked her lungs as she ran. She knew she should find a pace she could sustain for the whole fifteen hundred meters. But if she went fast now, she could feel, for about a hundred meters anyway, like a real runner. A fast runner. Someone with sprinter's genes.

Then she fell behind. Way behind.

Still, Ruthie ran. She ran as fast as she could. She ran until she felt as if a knife were lodged in her side. She ran until she felt nauseous. She ran until she crossed the finish line, last, so far behind the other girls that the parents had already surged down to the track to hug their winning daughters. Ruthie had to push through the small crowd to finish the race.

She didn't stop running then, either. She ran right out of the track gates and up to the top of the hill. Finally, panting, she collapsed on the grass. In the distance, on the lower field that was full of potholes and weeds, Joel and his friends had already begun playing football. All Ruthie wanted was to wipe out the feeling of that race, to annihilate the picture of jubilant parents hugging their fast, slim daughters. After catching her breath, she stood up and walked down to the lower field.

"I'll block for you," she told Joel.

He looked surprised, so taken off guard that he didn't smart-mouth anything, only said, "Okay."

Some of the other boys grumbled. A couple of them laughed. But in fact, Joel's team was one player short. So they shrugged, and someone said, "As long as she doesn't get in the way."

But Ruthie knew exactly what to do. She had studied the players' moves on TV. She blocked for Joel. She took the hits. She was good at it, too, and Joel ran twenty-two yards, then another ten. On fourth down, he scored a touchdown.

Ruthie's arms, legs, and sides hurt, but the ache felt good. With football, there's a reason for running. There's wind and mud. The autumny smell of grass. The tangle of bodies. Her own body became part of a big strategy, bigger even than the game she was playing. It was as if she had not only found the passageway out of the cave, but blown the top off.

When her team got the ball again, Ruthie spoke up in the huddle. "I want to go deep this time. Joel, let someone block for *me*."

"As if," one boy said.

"Oh, yeah right," another groaned.

"Let's do it!" Joel piped up, flashing his devil grin, the one the teachers hated. "It'll totally throw them off. They'll never expect it."

Joel dropped to his knees and used his finger to draw imaginary lines on the grass. He showed Ruthie where to begin blocking for him, as a fake, and then where to take off running long. The quarterback would hand off to Joel. He would fake as if he were going to run but quickly lateral the ball back to the quarterback, who would then pass to Ruthie.

It had been her idea, but now she shook her head. Her legs ached from running. Her chest hurt from taking hits and from sucking the cold air. Being a receiver was very different from blocking.

She tried to find her voice to say she had changed her mind, but Joel gave her a shove toward the scrimmage line.

She got down on a knee. The center hiked the ball. Joel ran behind the quarterback and took the handoff. That's when Ruthie felt her entire body rivet to attention. She didn't even have to think. She blocked for Joel, pushing aside two boys, then took off running long.

Ruthie wasn't fast, but she surprised the boys. For a few moments, no one took off after her. She turned to look for the pass, and there it was. A perfect spiral heading her way. Ruthie panicked. The ball was coming fast. She pushed her legs to go faster, stretch longer.

She lifted her arms and reached, just like the Niners' wide receiver. Her fingers touched the ball, and she gripped. It was hers, the football was hers.

Ruthie ran. Joel had caught up to her and was now at her side, sweeping the field, clearing her path. But the pack of boys was gaining on her, and he couldn't handle all of them. One dove at her legs. He wrapped his arms around her ankles. She tried to kick him off, but she was going down.

"Reach!" Joel shouted as she fell. So she did. She reached her arms in front of her, thrusting the football across the end-zone line as her face slammed into the hard, weedy ground.

Joel shot both arms high and parallel in the air. "Touch-down!" he shouted.

Then he dropped to his knees beside Ruthie and gently touched her cheekbone where a bruise would soon appear. "You okay?" he asked. She rolled over on her side and looked up at him. Briefly she saw the face of a boy who loved football more than he loved being mean. She fought back her welling tears, conquered them, and jumped to her feet.

A moment later, Ruthie was on the line of scrimmage, ready to play defense.

LUCY JANE BLEDSOE

Lucy Jane Bledsoe made her mark on women's sports history when she was in high school in Portland, Oregon. "I worked very hard to get the Portland Public Schools to comply with Title IX," she says. "They did comply, and by my senior year we finally had a girls' basketball team. I was most proud because my team won the Oregon State Championship that year."

Lucy grew up playing basketball, softball, tennis, and football, and she now takes part in cycling, back-country skiing, and kayaking. She's a fan of "all WNBA players" and Martina Navratilova. She says that for her, sports are about "learning to love our female bodies, especially in a culture that promotes such a narrow definition of acceptable female body types." That, plus her fascination with the "intensely physical aspects of team sports," led her to develop the character of Ruthie.

A full-time writer, Lucy recently spent three months in Antarctica as the recipient of a grant from the National Science Foundation Antarctic Artists and Writers Program. She has written a number of books, including novels for middle-grade readers: The Big Bike Race *(1995, about cycling);* Tracks in the Snow *(1997, about wilderness survival);* Wildcat Canyon *(2001, about mountain lions); and* Hoop Girlz *(2001, about basketball). Lucy also teaches in the graduate creative-writing program at the University of San Francisco. She lives in Berkeley, California.*

JUNE A. ENGLISH

Balance

My younger sister, Sheila, lives about eight miles down the road from me now. It's hard to miss Sheila. She has a mane of wild red hair, and she's nearly six feet tall. We don't know why her hair is red or how she got to be that tall. My father is no more than five-eleven, even when he stretches, and my mom is even shorter. Virtually no one in our family has had red hair in a hundred years. Well, there was my aunt Ethel. She had carrot red hair once, but only for a week.

I used to tease Sheila that she was adopted. I knew she wasn't, of course, since I was older. After she came home—about the fifth day, I think—I demanded that they return her to the hospital. She was a screamer from day one. When she was about three months old, I stuffed a wad of tissue paper in her mouth to keep her quiet. It wasn't a popular move, but it was one I kept considering through the years.

We shared a room and, like most sisters, had some dif-
ferences of opinion—that would be the polite way of
putting it. I made my bed most days, and the sheets were
generally washed and fairly tidy. My sister, on the other
hand, would require an archaeologist with carbon-dating
expertise to figure out how old some of the stuff was under
her bed. Baseball gloves, hockey pucks, and copies of *Sports
Illustrated* were all mixed in with about a month's worth of
laundry. Amid this more or less normal debris were about
fifteen assorted jars of dirt from Wrigley Field and several
other "incredibly important" ballparks Sheila had visited.
The entire effect was like a World War I trench inhabited
by a baseball team.

My sister kept her favorite bat lodged just above her pillow, even though once or twice I'm sure she got a concussion
bouncing on the mattress at the end of the day. I thought she
kept it there for protection, but I found out eventually that
she thought of it more like a wooden teddy bear.

Sheila was ten or so when she started playing baseball.
We both started, actually, but I was a dismal failure. I could
never seem to see the ball unless it came close enough to
knock me unconscious. Sheila, on the other hand, had all
the necessary skills to play the game. She could hit the ball,
run like lightning, and, most important, she could get
incredibly dirty. At times she was so dirty, she could have
been sold as real estate. That's the truth.

My dad got us a new truck in December of 1994. I had
just learned how to drive, and one of my jobs was to ferry
Sheila around. I would pick her up after practice—hoping
that most of the sweat would bounce off her before she
got in the seat. One day she came bounding up to the truck,

bat in one hand, glove in the other, with a doughnut in her mouth. It was an incredibly elegant presentation. She carefully nestled the glove and bat securely behind the seat and then stuck the honey-dipped doughnut on the dashboard.

"Do you think maybe you could find a napkin?" I asked.

"Not likely," she said, now trying to attach the doughnut to the gearshift.

"Is there any chance in our lifetimes that you'll clean yourself up?"

"I am clean. I'm just sweaty and dusty, like anybody'd be after playing for two hours. Besides, underneath all this stuff I'm just as clean as you are, maybe cleaner."

When I got home, I told my parents I wasn't picking Sheila up anymore. I told my father the experience was making me faint and I might just pass out behind the wheel. He smiled at me, but I could see he wasn't really amused.

"Part of the deal of you driving the truck is that you pick up Sheila."

"I wouldn't mind picking her up if she were like other people."

"Isn't she like other people?"

"No, she definitely isn't. She's six foot and every single foot of her is . . ." I danced around for a word while my father looked intense. He had—basically—a thirty-second limit on any argument involving my sister and me.

"You and your sister may be chalk and cheese, but this world is big enough for both of you."

The world maybe was, if we included both hemispheres, but one room was really pushing it.

. . .

When I walked upstairs, Sheila had taken a shower. There was a puddle trail from the bath into our room.

"Did you ever think of using a towel?"

"There was only one towel. I wrapped my hair in it."

She was lying in bed, rolling around to dry off.

"By the way, you don't have to pick me up on Wednesday. Mom and Dad are coming to see the game. Our Bluebirds are playing the Pelicans. The Pelicans won the league championship last year."

"Which league is that, the league of ornithologists?"

"You could come too if you wanted."

"I think I have to write a paper on the mating habits of the dodo."

"Suit yourself."

On Wednesday night—and need I say against my will?—I was sitting in the bleachers watching Sheila's Bluebirds battle the Pelicans.

Sheila typically played the outfield, left or center. Today she was stationed deep in center. The Pelicans—she had informed us in great detail—had a lot of long-ball hitters. Sheila, true to form, was catching everything that came within her range. She even snagged a few feathers from one of the pigeons that flew over her head.

It was the bottom of the eighth, and the Pelicans—who were never far behind—were threatening. A walk and a double had left Pelicans on second and third. Another long ball and the Bluebirds would lose their lead. Sheila, who had played the game near the fence, closed in on the infield.

"She hates when she can't play deep," said my father knowingly. Unlike the rest of us, he understood Sheila.

The Bluebird pitcher was tense. She was chewing her gum especially hard and blowing large bubbles between pitches. On a 3 and 0 count, she let go with a high hard one. The Pelican batter smacked at the ball, which was high enough to drop behind Sheila. She ran back for it, her long arm reaching. I could almost see her willing it into her glove. As she grabbed it she stumbled on a clump of grass. I expected her to fall, but somehow she didn't. Even without the ground to rely on, she balanced herself, pivoted, and in one elegant movement powered the ball to home plate. The catcher had plenty of time to block the plate and tag the runner.

My parents, as well as everyone else, were on their feet, raving. People were shouting Sheila's name. I sat on the bleachers, wondering: how did she do that? How could she pivot and throw that ball, without a foot on the ground?

We got home and had Sheila's favorite snack: Mountain Dew and Doritos. Dad promised her she could drive the tractor the next day.

Dad had a new John Deere combine that he used mostly, but he kept his old tractor around "just in case." Sheila would take it out now and then, running it over the fields when they were seeding. He only let her use it on flat ground. The Beast—as he called it—had a tendency to bank wildly.

Sheila was up early and out the door. Dad had left even earlier to see about something at the farm up the road.

Sheila started the Beast herself. The thing shook the ground like an angry brontosaurus. Ma was making breakfast and singing to herself. She was breaking eggs in a pan when we heard a noise like a shot. We stared at each other and started to laugh. The Beast was at least thirty years old. We figured the engine had just shut down. When we stopped laughing, though, we could still hear the grinding of gears.

"Go out there and see what's going on with that thing. And tell your sister to come in for breakfast. Tell her to leave that Beast alone till your dad comes back."

I ran out the back door to the little hill behind our house. I could see the old tractor, but it had rolled over and was turned on its side. I screamed for Ma and ran to see where Sheila was. As soon as I got near the cab, I saw that she was still inside. I climbed up on the side of the tractor.

Her face was turned away from me. "Get out of there," I said, knocking my fist on the glass window. When she turned toward me, I could tell she was in trouble. Her face was white—gray-white—like dirty snow, framed in a tangle of her red hair.

My mother was behind me now. "Get your father," she said, and pushed me hard in the direction of the neighbor's field.

I ran as fast as I could. My lungs hurt with the effort, and I thought furiously how Sheila could have run so much faster. I found my father but was so out of breath I had no voice. I just said, "Sheila," and started to cry.

We got in the neighbor's truck. On the way I started breathing again and told him she was still in the tractor. We drove fast down the road, and I felt myself sweating in the seat. The rivers of it rolled off my legs, and I could see the sweat on my father's temples. When we got back to the tractor, my mother had gotten the passenger side open and was holding Sheila's hand.

"Her leg is caught," my mother said, staring hard at my father. "She's in a lot of pain."

As if in agreement, Sheila let out a long moan. I never had heard her in pain before. It sounded terrible.

My dad was shaking his head, like he was trying to clear it to think. "I can't do this myself," he said. "I might hurt her worse. Call the paramedics. Tell them we might need something to get through metal. Tell them it's an old tractor."

We waited there with Sheila for the long minutes before the paramedics came with a fire truck. The firefighters cut through the metal, and they slowly pulled Sheila out of the tractor. Her legs were dangling at strange angles, and one was bleeding. They put her neck in a brace and strapped her legs to a board.

When they put her in the ambulance, she had IVs hanging off of her and was still so white, I thought she was going to die for sure. I looked hard at one of the paramedics as they loaded her into the ambulance. He must have known what I was thinking. "She'll be okay," he said. "It's all right."

I don't know if they are trained to say stuff like that, but it made me feel better. Ma and Dad went with the ambulance, but they made me stay home "in case something happens." I couldn't believe it. I wanted to go with Sheila. I sat staring at the blank television screen for two hours before they called to say Sheila was going to be all right.

She had broken bones in both her legs and crushed an ankle, but they could fix her.

I had dreamed so many times of having the room we shared to myself. That night I had my wish, but I couldn't sleep without her being there. I found myself staring at that baseball bat above her pillow. Eventually I fell asleep on her bed.

The next day my parents took me with them to the hospital. Sheila was still white, but she looked less slushy and was even smiling a little. It was startling to see her with casts on both her legs. And even more startling to see her so clean.

"Dad said you're going to have to take a defensive driving course before he lets you use another of his tractors."

Sheila laughed. The rocking of her body, though, sent a spasm of pain through her and she grimaced a little.

"Do you want me to bring you your baseball bat so you have something to hug at night?"

"Maybe you better wait," said Sheila. She looked tired. I sat next to her bed for a while, eating the hospital Jell-O she'd left on her dinner tray. "They said it will be months before I can even walk."

"Well, that's normal. I mean . . . you did really break some stuff."

"Actually, what they said was that one of my legs may be a little short."

"You're too tall anyway. What's an inch or two?"

I thought that was funny, but Sheila didn't laugh. She just shut her eyes and said she wanted to sleep. I went down to the lobby and found my parents. We got in the car and started the long drive back to the farm. The silence in the car made me uncomfortable.

"Sheila says she may end up shorter. I told her that might be an improvement."

My father gave me a hard look. I looked at my mother for a reprieve.

"Her ankle was crushed," she said. "They don't think they can fix it to be exactly the same."

"They can fix it, though," I said. "She'll be able to walk and everything."

My father stared straight ahead. His voice was quiet, but there was this tiny shake in it. "She can't run anymore."

I sat back in the car seat and looked out the window. I tried to picture Sheila not running in my mind, but that picture wouldn't come. Instead I kept seeing the image of Sheila catching that fly ball and pivoting on thin air.

A week later Sheila was home. For the next six months she went every week to rehab, where they taught her how to walk again. She was brave about it and determined, although she wouldn't go to the games anymore. Ma and Dad kept encouraging her to go—just to see her friends. But she kept shaking them off. The baseball season ended, and through the winter Sheila kept up her rehab. Her legs got stronger, but she had a slight limp, and the doctors told her she would have to get some corrective shoes to compensate for the shortness in her left leg.

By spring Sheila could walk around almost like a normal person. She didn't have all that much to entertain herself, though, so she cut her hair and began painting her nails. She even started cleaning her room. I think she thought I would appreciate her effort, but it kind of unbalanced me.

I found myself throwing my clothes around so the place would look normal again.

The coach at school kept calling, asking Sheila to come to the Bluebirds' opening game. She refused at first, but eventually she grudgingly said okay. We all went with her. I watched Sheila's face as all the Bluebirds lined up before the game and wondered how it could be that she wasn't standing with them. She seemed okay, though, staring straight ahead and clapping for them as they took the field. We sang the national anthem, and the coach came out and introduced the players. He said he'd like someone to throw out the first ball of the season. Then he brought the ball over to the stands and handed it to Sheila.

I don't think I ever saw Sheila drop a ball before, but she dropped that one. She dug it up out of the dirt, though, and walked to the mound. She stood there for a while in silence, and we all wondered if maybe this was just too much for her. But she finally kicked her leg up, drew back her arm, and let the ball fly. It was a clean strike.

Sheila never became a real pitcher. Her leg wouldn't allow her to cover first base fast enough. She did pitch relief in a couple of games, though, and ended up with a winning record. By the close of the season I had a boyfriend and I took him to watch one of the Bluebirds' last games. The game went into extra innings, and Sheila pitched the last two. He studied her on the mound for a while, her hands tarred up and her red hair flying. Finally he shook his head and laughed. "Your sister's nothing like you," he said. "I can't believe it."

I had heard that so many times in my life and never knew what to say. This time, though, I didn't even have to think about it.

"True, but there's room enough for both of us," I said, "even in just this hemisphere."

JUNE A. ENGLISH

June A. English says one of her proudest athletic achievements was making a basket from center court. "Unfortunately, it was during a volleyball game," she adds. "I hit the volleyball right through the hoop." Although June admits that her sports experience has been mostly as a spectator, she is a big baseball and horse-racing fan. She grew up near Maryland's Pimlico Race Course and had friends whose family trained racehorses. "I also started photographing horse races in college," she says. "I once got a photograph of Triple Crown winner Affirmed with all four legs off the ground."

June's story "Balance" grew out of the childhood experience of sharing a room with her sister, Patricia, who is ten years older than she is. "I am sometimes amazed at how different siblings can be from each other," she says.

Typically writing about environmental and space science as well as history, June has written more fiction of late and is currently working on a family memoir. Her books include Encyclopedia of the United States at War *(1998) and* Mission: Earth *(1996), both written with Thomas D. Jones;* The Most Dangerous Jobs in the U.S.A. *(1998); and* Transportation: Automobiles to Zeppelins *(1995), which was chosen for a Parents' Choice Award. June also won an Educational Press Association award for her short story "I Was a Child Volcano." She lives in Roxana, Delaware.*

GRACE BUTCHER

The Day the Horses Came

She galloped and trotted and walked and snorted and pranced and whinnied and bucked. She wasn't a horse; she was a girl who was a horse. Her legs were the horse, and the rest of her was her. The neighbors could see her on any given day, galloping over the rolling lawn, her braided mane bouncing. Her snorts and whinnies sounded very real.

Being in love with horses, for that's what she definitely was, had all started on Grandma and Grandpa's farm when she was very, very small—maybe five or six. She'd go with Grandpa to the little barn, and he'd hitch up big brown Champ to the disk and hoist her up onto Champ's broad back, and off they'd go to the field, Grandpa holding Champ's reins till they got there and Mary Kate just sitting there, little as anything and happier than anyone else, feeling Champ's strong body moving under her, carrying her along. When they got to the field that needed to be disked,

Grandpa would put the reins in her hands and say, "Okay, now, just go up and down, up and down the field till it's all disked up smooth and nice." And away he'd go to hoe the potatoes or cut some wood.

She never worried about being left all alone with such an important job. She never worried that Champ might suddenly decide to run away, dragging the disk behind him, and she might fall off. Happy in the hot sun, smelling Champ's good, sweet hot horse smell, tiny on his back but with the reins securely in her hands, she knew what to do. And Champ knew what to do. Together they did their job, and when they were done—Grandpa always seemed to know when that was and would appear at the edge of the field just as they finished the very last part—she'd ride Champ back to the barn and help Grandpa unbuckle the harness, dark sweat marks on Champ's shiny brown coat where the harness had rested. And then she'd put oats in his box by the pasture fence and watch him eat, and if Grandpa cut her a piece of an apple with his pocketknife, she'd hold her hand flat with the apple on it for Champ to take with his big lips, very softly.

Then time went by, and she moved away with her folks to another state where her dad had a job and she got to see Champ only once in a while when they'd go back to visit. She was ten now, and in her own big yard she galloped and trotted and snorted and whinnied and pretended to be a horse. She cut out pictures of horses from magazines and pasted them onto cards and kept a file of all her horses and drew pictures of the big horse barn she pretended to own.

And then one day Grandpa called her to tell her Champ had died. He was old and he just died. Grandpa said he'd get another horse, but she didn't listen and just put the phone hard into her mother's hand and walked away, crying. Later that day, feeling sort of sick and empty, she went out across the yard to her imaginary barn and chose from her many horses the one that looked most like Champ. She just walked him slowly back and forth, back and forth, as if they were disking up Grandpa's field so he could plant corn. And when they were finished, she slid down from his back, unhitched him the way Grandpa had always done, and then, standing on tiptoe to reach his head, took off his bridle and turned him loose. Champ trotted away, slowly disappearing, like a brown shadow, a brown ghost, fading, growing smaller up the far slope of the lawn, pausing once to look back at her for a long time before he vanished forever.

Maybe a year had gone by when an unexpected thing happened. Her birthday was coming soon, and to her amazement, her mother asked her, "Would you like to take riding lessons?" Mary Kate could hardly answer, she was so excited. A little riding stable had opened up down the road about a mile or two. It was just a little cement-block barn, and the horses didn't have much room in their stalls, and the owners, Marge and Bill, were sort of gruff, shabby people, she thought at first, and she felt shy around them. The stable was in the country, and the riding ring was outdoors in a huge field by the river. It had no fences around it and wildflowers and high grass grew in the middle and a dirt path was worn in the grass around the edge where the horses were ridden. It was so big that anyone riding there could pretend to be out on the trail or in the wilderness or on the vast prairie. And through a little opening in the bushes, you could ride your horse right to the river and sit on him while he drank, just like in the movies.

And the first time she went there, she fell in love. For her first lesson, Bill said, "I have just the horse for you," and went away down a hill out of sight. When he came back, he was leading the most beautiful horse in the world. "This is Star," Bill said. "I think you'll like him. He's from out west."

Star was black as anything. His coat shone in the sun like coal. And his mane was so thick and long, it stood out against his big neck as if it were electric and had a life of its own. His tail was as thick as his mane and hung nearly to the ground. And on his forehead, the small white mark for which he was named. He wasn't too tall, a just-right size for her to climb onto him without any help, and his legs were chunky and strong looking, like all the rest of his body.

When Star was saddled and she got on, Bill walked with her down to the riding ring, where some other kids on horses were waiting. They all started around the edge of the big field in a line. She sat proudly and kept her back straight and her hands and feet just so, the way Bill showed them as he rode his own horse alongside them.

"Now we're going to trot," Bill said. "Give your horse a little kick in the sides with your heels." Star and all the other horses started trotting, and Mary Kate started bouncing so hard on the saddle, she didn't know what to do. Her teeth even hit together, she bounced so hard. Champ had never trotted except when Grandpa hitched him to the wagon and they went trotting down the dirt road by the farm with Grandpa holding the long reins and Mary Kate beside him, holding on to the edge of the rough wooden seat. But when Star trotted, she was shocked at bouncing around so hard and feeling like he didn't want her in the saddle.

But then Bill rode up to her on his horse and told her to "stand up in the stirrups and sit down and stand up and sit down," and that had never occurred to her, so she tried to do that: ". . . up . . . down . . . up . . . down," he said. "That's it. One . . . two . . . one . . . two . . . ," and clutching Star's thick mane and the front of the saddle, she stood up a little and sat down hard and bounced for several steps, and then stood up again and sat down . . . and suddenly her body felt the rhythm of the horse's quick steps, and she stopped her frantic, sloppy bouncing and began to rise and fall in a sort of duet with Star: left . . . right . . . left . . . right he went, and up . . . down . . . up . . . down she went, and it was so smooth that when Bill said to everybody, "Walk!" loudly so they all could hear him, she was startled, and then disappointed, and then she couldn't wait till he said, "Trot!" again so she could go along in this dance with Star, her thigh muscles lifting her and setting her down, her rear end barely touching the saddle oh so softly before she'd lift herself again. Her legs felt so strong from all her own trotting and galloping on her imaginary horses—so strong, just like Star's legs.

She got off when they were done and gave him an apple and watched as Marge and Bill took him and the other horses back to the pasture again, and then she got into the car with her mother. She tried to tell her mother about the way she'd felt as if she were dancing with the horse, but it was hard to find the words, though her mother nodded and smiled as if she understood.

Twice a week that summer, her mother drove her to the stable or she rode her bike there. She learned the names of all the horses and that you could ask for the one you wanted, and so she always asked for Star. But after a couple of weeks of happily walking and trotting around the big field, usually on Star but sometimes on Wild Honey with the reddish freckles or Chief, who was plain brown, kind of like old Champ had been, something happened.

Bill said, "Today we're going to canter. Once you're trotting, give your horse a little kick." After a few trotting steps, Mary Kate touched Star's sides with her heels. Star suddenly lurched forward, catching her so by surprise that she nearly toppled over backward onto his rump. Then his hindquarters rose abruptly and flung her forward, both arms wrapped around his neck. Her face was in his long thick mane, and then she felt herself sliding sideways, sliding down over his shoulder, and suddenly she lost her grip on his neck and landed with an awful thump in the soft dirt right beside his flying feet. The horse behind them just missed stepping on her. She hardly knew what had happened, it was all over so fast.

Bill jumped off his horse and squatted down beside her. "Are you okay?" he asked.

"Yes," she said, not quite sure but scrambling to her feet. She felt funny, as if her whole body were buzzing, and her elbow hurt a little where she'd landed on it, and her clothes were all brown and dusty from the dirt she'd landed in.

When the line of horses came by, Star with them, Bill helped her climb back up into the saddle. "Try again. You can do it!" he said.

She sat high in the air on her beloved Star, who had so betrayed her, and she was trembling and very fearful. Did she really have to do it again?

She did. "Canter!" and the horrible lurching started again. How could this be riding? This was no fun. Why would anyone want to do this? And she hung on to the saddle and her thighs ached with trying to cling to Star's sides, and her throat felt tight, like she wanted to cry. She wished the lesson were over! She wished she were on her bike riding up the road toward home. It had never occurred to her to fall off one of her imaginary horses. She wished she were five years old again on Champ in the slow, hot summer on the farm.

And again, after a walk that was much too short—"Canter!" She was so sad at this awful thing that Star was doing to her that after a couple of bounds and a couple of bruising bangs from the saddle on her very unhappy bottom, she just gave up. She stopped trying to hang on and just sat there like a lump, not caring whether her body was forward or backward or where it was.

And suddenly it was just right. She found herself sitting in the saddle as if Star were a rocking chair. Her back was straight and supple, and her hips moved as if one with the great swoops and arcs the horse's body made as he loped along on the soft dark earth of the path. Oh! she thought. Oh! This is how you do it! She swung along completely in his rhythm and felt as if she had always known how to do this wonderful thing. She thought her whole body must be glowing, as if a great light were around the two of them. They seemed to be all alone in a world where there was nothing to do but for Star to canter with her on his back forever.

When she wasn't at the riding stable, she cut out more pictures of horses, each with its own personality, and put them in their imaginary stalls in her imaginary barn. Under each picture she wrote about the traits of each horse. Some of these horses were wild, and you could see them trying to buck her off at a pretend rodeo, but she tamed them all and the imaginary audience would applaud wildly. All the horses came to love her. They high-stepped around the yard, did tricks for her. They kicked out with their heels, which were, of course, her heels, and Mary Kate and her invisible horses ran and ran.

The problem was that she wanted her own horse. Not just any horse. Only Star. But her father said, "No. We have no barn, no pasture, not enough money now to buy and feed a horse and put shoes on his feet and a saddle on his back. No."

"But Dad . . ."

"No. Who's going to take care of it? Your mother and I don't know anything about horses."

"I'm twelve now. I know how to take care of a horse," she insisted. "I helped Grandpa take care of Champ when I was just a little kid. I help Bill and Marge down at the riding academy. They say I'm the best rider down there. They say I have a way with horses. They let me go over jumps and take riders out on the trail and clean the stalls and brush the horses. All the horses like me. I've read books about horses and how to take care of them. I know how to. . . ."

"No," her dad said. "Besides, Star belongs to them and they need him there and he's not for sale." And that was that.

She'd always loved her dad. But now she felt so sad and angry that she didn't even feel like talking to him or doing anything with him that they used to do. She galloped wildly around the yard even in the dark. The moon was a spotlight, and the white horse she was riding shone silver in the moonlight and had stars tangled in its mane.

"What's the matter with her?" her father would say to her mother. And her mother, who did, after all, know more about her love of horses than her dad, would just shake her head or shrug and continue cooking supper or reading a book.

The day the horses came, it was early in the morning. She'd awakened way before she usually did, for some reason. Or she thought she had. Maybe she was still asleep and hearing her mother's voice in a dream, telling her to look out on the lawn. She went to her bedroom window. Maybe I am awake, maybe not, she thought. Three horses were peacefully grazing on the short grass of the well-mowed lawn. They were all from the riding stable. One was Charlie, dark brown and lanky. One was Prince, brown-and-white spotted. And the third one was Star. Star? Was he a dream or was he real?

How could they be on her lawn? How long had they been there? She had never ridden Star to her house; that wouldn't have been allowed. How did he and the others get out of their pasture more than a mile away? How did they know to come here? She could hardly believe her eyes. While her mother called the stable owners, she threw on her clothes, put some oatmeal in a little pan, and walked out the door toward them, shaking the oats gently so they made a good sound for the horses. Star lifted his head, took a step toward her, reached out for the pan of oats. She took hold of his halter and let him eat, taking a handful out for Charlie and Prince when they crowded in to see what Star was getting.

Bill and Marge came up the road in their old car. Bill dropped Marge off, and she put lead lines on Charlie and Prince but brought a bridle for Mary Kate to put on Star. Mary Kate wiggled up onto his broad bare back, and they all started slowly back down the road. She'd ridden him bareback many times before and loved the feeling of nothing between her body and his but her jeans and his satiny smooth black coat.

As they went along the side of the road, Marge told her that the pasture fence, rickety at best, had sagged till a section had fallen down and the trio must have just walked over it sometime during the night.

"But why did they come to my house?" Mary Kate asked her. "How did they know where I lived?"

"I don't know," Marge said. "It must have been fate. Maybe you and Star are supposed to be together."

The ride seemed over too quickly, and when Mary Kate slipped off Star's back and led him to his stall, she lingered there, leaning up against him, smelling his good smell, listening to the sounds he made as he ate some hay from his manger—the swish and rustle as he pulled the hay free, the crunching as he chewed.

"Your mom's here," Marge yelled from the barn door.

And slowly Mary Kate walked out into the bright early morning sun and over to the car. "Mom, Star came to my house," she said as they drove home. "How did he know where I live?"

Her mother shook her head. "Magic, I guess."

Mary Kate smiled. "That's what I think, too. Mom, couldn't we buy him? He doesn't have a good life there. They let anybody ride him, and I saw some guy hit him with a stick to make him go faster, and once Charlie kicked him, and he won't go over jumps for anybody but me, and he follows me to the river to drink—I don't even need a rope to lead him, and he comes when I call him, and—"

"Stop!" her mother said. "You know what your dad said. We have no barn, no pasture—"

"He could live in the garage and eat the grass on the lawn and you wouldn't have to mow it and—"

"No. You can go down there nearly every day and ride him."

"But sometimes I can't. Bill and Marge let other people take him out, and they just make him run all the time out on the trail and even up and down the hills, and you're not supposed to do that!"

Her mother was silent when they pulled in the driveway, and Mary Kate spent the rest of the day riding four or five of her imaginary horses but making them all just walk and slowly trot because she was sad and didn't feel like galloping. Late that night she thought she heard her mom and dad arguing downstairs, but she fell asleep thinking about how gleaming black Star had looked in the slant of early morning sun, the dark hoofprints on the dewy lawn where he had walked.

・ ・ ・

The rest of the summer she rode Star when she could and turned away in anger when she saw other people on him. She helped Bill and Marge clean the barn and brush down the horses when they'd rolled in the mud. She didn't talk to her dad much, and when he asked her if she'd like to play catch or go for a bike ride, she always said no and ran off to her imaginary barn to saddle up one of her imaginary horses. After she said no to her dad, she'd gallop wildly, bucking and kicking, needing all her skill to stay on and all her strength on the invisible reins to keep her invisible mount from running away with her.

Her parents argued more and more, but always after she'd gone to bed, and she couldn't hear what they were saying, just the angry sound of their voices drifting like a dark wind up the stairs and down the hall past her closed door.

At school while the other girls played basketball on the playground or sat on the steps and laughed and talked, she did a strange thing. She jogged around the far edges of the playground, in and out among the trees that ringed the field. She just jogged slowly like a runner warming up, but what she was really doing was riding the invisible dapple gray horse she'd ridden to school that morning, galloping alongside the school bus with magic speed, keeping up with it easily, jumping ditches and fences, while her friends stared out the window, amazed and envious.

There always seemed to be a sort of window between her and the other kids. Oh, she had friends, but she was different from them somehow. None of them seemed to live in the same kind of world she did, where what was real and what she could imagine were almost the same thing. Almost. But no matter how hard she imagined her horses, they were never really there, the way Champ had been, the way Star was now, except as she felt them in her legs and in the flow of her long hair in the wind of her own galloping. And she felt very lonely sometimes.

"Hey, Mary Kate, come play with us!" the girls shooting baskets called to her. "We need one more person!"

"No, I feel like running," she would shout back. And when recess was over, she tied her invisible horse to a tree where it would wait for her till the school bus headed out, and then she'd ride back home again.

One of the best things about going to the riding stable after school was that after she'd been out on Star or cleaning his stall or brushing him or the other horses, all the good special horse smell would be on her for a long time. And when she was in the house, she'd take a sniff of her bare arm and say out loud to no one in particular, "Oh, I smell like a horse!" and she'd make a little "ummm" of delight.

"Doesn't that girl ever wash?" she heard her dad say, sounding very annoyed, to her mom in the kitchen one night. She didn't hear her mother's reply, but she thought that maybe—just maybe—her mother had been a horse, too, a long time ago, because her mother never seemed to think all her galloping and whinnying was strange. Sometimes Mary Kate saw her mother watching her trotting and prancing and bucking and snorting around their vast, rolling lawn that had probably been a pasture once before the house was built there—and she thought maybe her mother smiled now and then to see her horsey little girl jumping over the garden bench and tossing her mane.

One day Mary Kate tried again with her dad while he was reading the Sunday funnies. They used to sprawl on the floor together, and he'd read them to her till she'd gotten old enough to read them herself. But then they'd still lie on the floor together and laugh. Not now, though. Not since he didn't understand anything anymore. Not since he'd made her go take a bath and wash off the musky smell of the horse barn.

"Dad?" He looked up from the paper. "Listen—you remember the day the horses came here? Why do you think they came?" She talked faster. "Star brought them! How did he know where I lived? Why did he come here? It was magic!"

He looked back at the paper again. She rushed on. "It *was* magic! It *had* to be! Even Mom says it was magic, and Marge said it was fate. He wants to be with me and he belongs here!"

Her father put the paper down abruptly and stood up, towering over her. "I don't want to hear any more about it," he said, not loudly but in a way that made Mary Kate feel like his words had hit her in the stomach. And he started toward the stairs.

Suddenly she yelled at his back, "I hate you!" and as he turned around with a look of shock and then great sadness on his face, she ran outside and ran all the way down the road a mile or more to the stable, crying as she ran. She ran into the barn and up the stairs to where Bill and Marge lived above the stable right next to the hayloft. They were eating supper. The walls were bare cement blocks. Wisps of hay lay on the unswept floor.

"I want to live here with you!" she gasped out. "I'll work really hard and clean all the stalls, not just Star's, and I'll brush all the horses—okay?"

Bill and Marge looked at each other, startled. Marge said to her, "Sit down and have some meat loaf," and Bill went into the other room. She could hear him dialing the phone.

Sitting at the table, hearing the horses stamping in their stalls below, smelling the good barn smell everywhere, Mary Kate imagined how wonderful it would be to live in such a place, sharing your house with the horses, able to ride anytime day or night, nothing to do but take care of the horses, feed them, take them to the river to drink, hold them while the blacksmith shaped new shoes for them in his red-hot forge. Marge gave her a glass of milk in an old jelly jar.

But soon enough her mother drove up outside, and Marge took her downstairs. "You must not do this again, or we won't be able to let you ride here anymore. Your parents are good folks. You don't want to make them worry about you."

Her mother didn't say anything as they drove home, and her father must have already gone to bed. The house was very quiet. She looked out her bedroom window, trying to make Star appear on the lawn in the moonlight, but he wasn't there. He was at the stable in his stall, and she hadn't even put her arms around his thick black neck that night.

A few weeks went by. She rode Star when she could and one of the other horses when she couldn't. Charlie was so tall and lanky and took such long steps she never felt in rhythm with him when he trotted. Prince felt like a car jouncing over a bumpy road when he cantered. Sunny always wanted to run away, the way he had when he'd been young and on the racetrack, and it took all her strength to hold him in. Dolly would spook and give a little buck for no apparent reason and never let her relax. Star was the only one who did everything right. He was the only really beautiful and perfect one.

At home she added stalls to the imaginary barn that she'd drawn on a big piece of brown wrapping paper and cut out more pictures of horses to put in them. She could gallop what seemed like forever without getting tired. Her breathing was easy and her legs were strong. Sometimes she undid her braids and let her mane fly in the wind. For days she had looked out the window every morning to see if Star had come again, but Bill had fixed the pasture fence so the horses couldn't get out. After a while she didn't look anymore. At the stable she could always tell when others had been riding him. She could feel his tiredness seep up into her own body, and there'd be white places on his neck where the sweat had dried. She was happy to let him just walk on those days, and sometimes she'd even slide off and walk beside him. They'd wander down to the river, where he'd suck up great gulps of the rushing water, then paw it with his foot, splashing them both. She'd pretty much resigned herself to having only this little bit of him in her life.

Her dad went to work and came home, went to work and came home. Things went on more or less as they always had. The truck with the load of lumber came to her house while she was at school, so she didn't know about the pile of boards in the garage. Her mom took her to buy some clothes and visit some relatives all day on Saturday, so she didn't hear the pounding in the garage where her dad was making something. And Sunday they all went for a long drive in the country to see the beautiful fall colors. She wasn't very interested in the scenery or in talking to her parents, but galloping alongside the car on her invisible horse gave her something to do: jump wide ditches, leap over road signs and mailboxes, stop when the car stopped, gallop off again when it started. She didn't even feel as if she were in the car at all. She was bareback on her huge, magnificent horse a few feet away. His coppery coat shone in the sun like a new penny. She felt sorry for her mom and dad, who didn't even know he was there, while people in other cars stared in amazement as they galloped by.

Back home hours later, she climbed quickly out of the car, eager to walk her imaginary horse till it cooled down, then see to it that it had fresh imaginary straw for bedding down in its stall. Her dad put the car in the garage and headed toward the house. As she was walking toward the invisible barn far across the big lawn, he called to her.

"Mary Kate, I left my keys in the car. Would you please go get them when you're ready to come in?"

"Okay," she called back, continuing to walk a little prancy walk across the yard. When you ran and jumped a horse the way she just had, you could expect it to take a while to quiet down. Finally putting her horse in its stall, she headed for the garage. Funny, she didn't remember her dad ever asking her to get his keys for him before. She went in the little side door and stopped dead.

It was a two-car garage, and there was the car, where it always was. But on the side that used to be empty, there was a stall of raw new wood. And in the stall, standing as quietly as if he had always stood there, was Star. This time he had come to stay.

That night she wrote a poem.

THE DAY THE HORSES CAME

The day the horses came,
something changed in the world.
Star brought his friends to visit me,
to show them where he belonged.
He led them here on a magic path.
They left their hoofprints in the dew.
He was so jet black in the golden sun
that he dazzled my eyes.

And now that he's here,
all my invisible horses have disappeared.
They will never come back,
and that is all right with me.
They have galloped away to be with
some other little girl who needs them.
They taught me. They made me strong.
I will always remember them.

Soccer

We are all longing for the ball.
It comes to one of us and then another.
It is so white against the green
you can still see it if you close your eyes.
Our bodies seem small in the vast stadium
whose walls are made of people.
They scream for us and at us,
telling us what to do as if we did not know.
We know the color of our shirts in our dreams,
take a long pass with barely a glance,
always know where teammates are.
Our feet dig and dance, our bodies
smash and tangle on the ground.
Our heads meet the ball in midair,
not an easy introduction.
Our muscles gleam with sweat.

We love our bodies,
how strong they are, our legs, the way
our thighs and calves ripple in the sun.

The goal is guarded as if in a fairy tale
by troll, by ogre, dragon. We shout
to each other, "Here!" and "Here!"
And the ball, as if alive, comes to our feet
when called. And now the dragon's fire is dim.
The ogre grows smaller.
The troll has gone into hiding.
Once upon a time we were not dragon slayers.
Look at us now!
The net opens like a mouth,
huge and hungry.
The ball goes in.

Basketball

When the ball slams hard and heavy
into my hand, and I lift off
for that layup,
the world shrinks into
one small circle,
and time stops
while I hang in the air.
The net holds nothing but stars
till the ball swishes through
and applause surges in
from the galaxies.
The net fills again with stars.
The whole gym seems full of light.
I feel as if I am shining.

Track

My track shoes
turn me into a cheetah.
My spikes are claws.
They strike sparks from stones;
they dig into the earth
and secure me to this
spinning planet.
They make me faster
than anyone.
The wind of my own running
puts tears of joy into my eyes.
I am a cheetah
made of wind and fire.

GRACE BUTCHER

Grace Butcher has been running track since 1949. She was the U.S. champion in the eight hundred meters (880 yards) three times and held the U.S. record in that event several times from 1958 to 1961. Since 1977 she's run the eight hundred in Masters competition; she won the silver medal in that distance at the World Masters Games in 1989.

Besides running track, Grace grew up swimming, bicycling, playing badminton, and riding horses, and an incident from her childhood was the inspiration for "The Day the Horses Came." Grace played varsity basketball in high school and took part in horse shows, motocross, and motorcycle road racing as an adult. The poems that Grace contributed to this anthology touch on her broad sports interests. She says she wrote "Soccer" with the U.S. women's 1999 World Cup victory in mind.

Grace has written three books of poetry for adults and was named Ohio Poet of the Year in 1992 for her book Child, House, World. *Her work has won an Ohio Arts Council creative-writing award and a National Endowment for the Arts award. She wrote a column on motorcycling for* Rider *magazine from 1979 through 1985, and her article on motorcycle touring and camping for* Sports Illustrated *has been reprinted in* Reader's Digest *and six high-school and college textbooks. Her poems have been reprinted in many anthologies, including* Best American Poetry 2000. *Grace is a professor of English (emeritus) at Kent State University, Geauga Campus. She is the mother of two grown sons and lives in Chardon, Ohio.*

PAT CONNOLLY

Women Will

Gasping for air I bend over
    to catch my breath.
Drop by drop the sweat of my brow
    spreads a darkening circle on the track.
I have pushed my heart and lungs
    and cramping muscles to exhaustion.

Gasping for air as needles and pins of doubt
    prick my soul and pierce
    my pounding disappointed heart.
I want to disappear like my sweat into the earth.

And then, a breeze that ripples stadium flags
    carries new breath from ancient gods.
I take the outstretched hand of the victor,
    sharing with her an eternal moment.
The agony and ecstasy of Olympia.

PAT CONNOLLY

Growing up, Pat Connolly loved swimming and tennis, but she made her mark in track and field. A three-time Olympian, Pat was sixteen years old when she ran the eight hundred at the 1960 games; in 1964 and 1968 she went on to compete in the pentathlon. Pat's Olympic eight-hundred-meter race inspired her to write "Women Will." "I was pushed to the ground and fell a hundred meters from the finish line," she says. "I'd never lost a race before, and I was quite shocked to find myself on the ground. But I made myself get up and finish." (Coincidentally, author Grace Butcher had been the defending U.S. champion in the eight hundred in 1960, but she missed the Olympics because of a broken foot.)

Now a cycling enthusiast, Pat shares her track experiences with young athletes as the director and head coach of the men's and women's track-and-field and cross-country teams at Radford University in Virginia. The former coach of Olympic sprinter Evelyn Ashford, Pat is the author of Coaching Evelyn: Fast, Faster, Fastest Woman in the World *(1991) and has contributed articles and a 1996 Olympic journal to* The New York Times. *She lives in Radford, Virginia.*